I0557678

The Only Real House of Mirrors

David S. Barkley

Published By: N. Simonson & Company, Los Angeles

Copyright © 2013 David S. Barkley
All rights reserved.

ISBN: 978-0-9891751-1-1

FOR MEIDY, STEP BY STEP

CONTENTS

CONTENTS (Continued)

ACKNOWLEDGMENTS

There are so many and you know who you are!

There at the beginning were:

Verne Tharpe, physical director of the YMCA in Racine Wisconsin. He taught me that geeks can do physical things.

James van Stone, Ph.D., Donald Galbraith, Ph.D. and Theodore Mauch, Ph.D., Professors of Biology and Religion, Trinity College, Hartford Connecticut. They showed me how to aim high and fall well.

John Bonner, Ph.D. and Malcolm Steinberg, Ph.D., Professors of Biology, Princeton University, Princeton, NJ. Daniel Atkinson, Ph.D., Professor of Chemistry, UCLA. They taught me how to think.

Judith Orloff, M.D and John Buksbazen, Psy.D., Los Angeles California. They taught me how to feel.

Michael DiGiovanni, Alan Thompson, Arthur Freilich, Kenneth Yates, Charles Boudakian, and Louis and Jo Furman. They kept me on the path.

Medias Hening Pratiwi. Without her, the final chapters would never have been written.

PROLOG

It's early afternoon as I hike into this high meadow and see the glacier. I've been alone on the trail for days but now, suddenly, there are carnival tents! She never said anything about this!

A barker sits in his cage and eyes me cautiously.

"What is this place?" I ask.

He points to red lettering on a bright yellow banner that announces: "The Only Real House of Mirrors." Smaller, black letters say, "Enter at your own risk."

"How much?" I ask.

He points to another sign.

"That's a lot," I complain.

Silence.

I pay the barker his fee, enter, and follow the tent curtains along a twisting passage. It's dark. Up ahead I see an exit at the back of the tent.

"That's it?"

Feeling chagrined I leave the tent and follow a path up towards the ice.

I look back only once; the tents are gone.

1 MARK

"Are you a Christian?"

It is a windless night and the only other sound is the hiss of butane from my small camp stove.

"No," I answer. "I'm a scientist. I left my superstitions behind me long ago."

I surprise myself with the bitterness in my words.

I arrived at this campsite quite late and it was already dark by the time I rolled out my sleeping bag, boiled water, and reconstituted a small box of freeze-dried tuna fish. The question comes as I am using the last of the water to make tea, and my attention has wandered from my task into that strange place where these voices seem to live.

This time there is no body attached to the voice — I appear to be alone in the camp.

"Are you angry?" the voice asks.

I can't answer. My voice chokes on the fear in the base of my throat. Tears fill my eyes, and I remember.

**

I was ten years old; confined to bed in a U.S. Army hospital in Tokyo. I didn't know why I was there, but I did know from the faces of the nurses that I was very sick. The day before the doctor had botched a spinal tap and the large bruise on my back conspired with my headache to make the world a totally miserable place in which to live. The room where I was confined contained four beds, but the other three were empty. No one had come through the door for several hours; the room was silent; lunch was at least an hour away; and there was no position for my body that offered any release from my suffering.

I was a serious child — my head filled with weighty matters — and I had been dwelling on something a Sunday school teacher had told me back in the States.

"Christ suffered and died on his cross for our sins," she said. "Only through his terrible pain are we redeemed."

"Terrible pain," I muttered, remembering those words from my hospital bed, "I'd have traded places with him in a minute. … He knew he was God. He had no doubts. He knew that after a few hours of physical torture he would go right back to being Ruler of the Universe."

Somehow Christ's contribution to my well-being seemed rather insignificant. My own doubts and fears were far greater than anything God could experience — even from a cross.

And that's when it happened. A terror washed over me that was greater than anything I had ever experienced in my ten years of life. I was an atheist! There was no God!! I was alone!!!

I cried that night and was sullen through most of the next day. My doctors thought I had had a relapse. I never told anyone the truth.

**

"So God has no doubts," the voice asserts.

"God doesn't exist," I reply.

"Don't be silly," the voice laughs. "You've read the Gospel of Mark. You know what it means."

**

This time the memory called up was quite pleasant. I was a freshman at a small, liberal arts college in New England. I was proud that I had been admitted. I felt important. I loved learning things.

The college still clung to the tatters of an ecclesiastical history, and all students were required to take at least one semester of religion. I had chosen a survey course of the Old and New Testaments of the Bible.

"The Bible has a history," my professor was saying, "and sometimes it doesn't make a lot of sense unless you know that history.

"The Gospels Mathew, Mark, Luke, and John were not written by the apostles of the same name, they were written later, by Christians trying to make sense of an event already turning to myth with the passage of time. Current scholarship suggests that Mark was written first — a decade or so after the death of Christ, perhaps by a friend of the apostle Peter. The other gospels were written later.

"If you want to meet the historical Jesus, read Mark."

I did read Mark, over and over again, in the course of that college semester. I followed Jesus along sun bright, dusty roads that were hot with human misery. The crippled, the diseased, the insane crowded around that man like a suffocating fog — his early acts of healing summoning even more people in terrible pain.

He seemed quite human to me, though blessed with remarkable skills. Perhaps he even seemed human to himself; Mark refers to him as the Son of Man.

Most of the words attributed to him from the cross come from other Gospels. In Mark he says, "My God, my God, why hast thou forsaken me." All is pain — no words with the thieves to his right and left, no promises that they will enter with him into paradise.

I remember feeling chills when I read Mark's last chapter:

> And when the Sabbath was past, Mary Magdalere, and Mary the mother of James, and Salome, brought spices, so that they might go and anoint him. And very early on the first day of the week they went to the tomb when the sun had risen. And they were saying to one another, "who will roll away the stone for us from the door of the tomb?" And looking up, they saw that the stone was rolled back; for it was very large. And entering the tomb, they saw a young man sitting on the right side, dressed in a white robe; and they were amazed. And he said to them, "Do not be amazed; you seek Jesus of Nazareth, who was crucified. He has risen, he is not here; see the place where they laid him. But go, tell his disciples and Peter that he is going before you to Galilee; there you will see him, as he has told you." And they went out and fled from the tomb; for trembling and astonishment had come upon them; and they said nothing to any one, for they were afraid. [1]

And there, to my astonishment, the Gospel ends! [2] No sightings of the resurrected Christ, no ascension into heaven. Just an empty tomb and three women too frightened to speak.

I sat very still the day my professor interpreted the words of the young man in the white robe. "He's not here," my professor quoted the young man. "Go back to Galilee, where you lived and where you worked. In your life there, you will find him."

**

While remembering these things a cold wind has started down the glacier and is striking my back with some force. My shirt is drenched with sweat and its chill is refrigerating. I can hear the wind.

"Are you a Christian?" asks my companion, a second time.

"Yes," I answer happily. "I'm a scientist. I left my superstitions behind me long ago."

"You still don't get it, do you." laughs my friend.

And so we spend the night telling stories — surrounded by mysteries, enchanted by sorrow.

"You still don't get it, do you." laughs my friend.

~~

[1] The Gospel According to Mark 16: 1–8 (The Holy Bible, Revised Standard Edition, Thomas Nelson & Sons, 1946, 1952).

[2] "Authorities" added verses 9–20 centuries later. Only verses 1–8 belong to the original text.

2 WIND

"This is nice!" I tell myself.

I am sitting on a narrow rock ledge, secured to a thousand foot wall of granite by a climber's harness, several lengths of one-inch tubular nylon, and three carefully placed wedges of metal alloy known to rock climbers as chocks. My feet dangle over the edge and, between them, far below; I see the boulder field that completely surrounds the high mountain lake where I camped last night. I've been sitting here for several hours. I watched the progress of two climbers coming up the wall slightly to my left until I lost them in the shadows that climbed the wall faster than they. I now sit — in the light of an almost full moon — listening to the wind.

**

"The Bible has a history, and sometimes it doesn't make a lot of sense unless you know that history. The oldest parts of the Old Testament are called the 'J' account, and they were assembled one thousand years before the birth of Christ by scholars in the court of King David. To read the 'J' account is to see the souls of a people who lived with

God on a daily basis. When they wrote about God they wrote about personal experience."

The professor was the same. The classroom was the same. The desk was the same.

"For example, in Modern Hebrew the word for 'wind' is 'ruach,' but it also has another meaning, 'Spirit of the Lord.'

"Take your choice!" he looked straight at me. "'And Abraham went up onto the mountain and the Spirit of the Lord came upon him' or 'And Abraham went up onto the mountain and the wind blew'."

He looked away. "Many Old Testament scholars will tell you that the authors of the Old Testament used such double meanings to craft magnificent poetry. … I will not."

He looked at me a second time. "Could it be that, three thousand years ago, 'ruach' had only one meaning? Could it be that, for those people at that time, the wind blowing across a mountaintop was identical to the presence of God … that there was no difference? Shepherds of ancient Israel, sitting on hillsides outside the walls of Jerusalem, had few scientific paradigms from which to assemble a map of the world. When the wind blew, they did not feel moving masses of air. When they looked at the night sky, they did not see planets, stars, and galaxies. Ancient people perceived wind and stars, if not directly, free at least of some layers of deliberately constructed abstraction.

"For those shepherds, and for the authors of the 'J' account of the Old Testament, the universe was a mystery that was continuously experienced as God!"

**

A gap of twenty years exists between that classroom and this narrow, moonlit ledge. Some of that gap is filled with maps constructed out of experiences in biology, chemistry, physics, and mathematics. The rest of the gap is filled by wind.

**

"… Dilute the virus suspension and add it to a young broth culture of sensitive bacteria. Wait two minutes, neutralize unabsorbed virus with appropriate antisera, dilute with warm broth, and then withdraw samples at regular intervals for assay of the number of plaque-forming units."

The blackboard behind my professor was filled with circles and arrows that together told the story of the life cycle of a bacterial virus called T2. This was graduate school and the teaching style was new to me. My professor had spent only the briefest of moments describing the life cycle of this magnificent machine. Virtually the entire three hour lecture was devoted to a recitation of specific experiments (along with names, dates, and university affiliation) — what had been done and what had been observed.

"… Notice that the smooth carpet of confluent bacterial growth is interrupted by visible, circumscribed areas that are perfectly clear. These plaques, as they are called, indicate …" [1]

We were learning the process by which scientists acquire new knowledge, and it was absolutely clear to me that the process was more important than the conclusion. I quickly fell in love with the process and began to play a private game. Every time one of my professors drew a conclusion from an experiment, I would try to draw a different conclusion. Sometimes I succeeded and sometimes I didn't. If I failed I would still feel that I could have drawn a different conclusion if only I had been a little smarter.

Gradually, however, I was overwhelmed by the sheer quantity of confident conclusion that suffused science.

One night, while walking alone on a quiet campus path, I recall assembling an elaborate thought experiment from small pieces of irrefutable, scientific fact. There was a moment of exquisite indecision when I remembered that some of these facts had seemed less certain when I first encountered them — time and repetition played an important role in their current, exalted status. For a moment, my ears roared and my stomach heaved as everything I knew seemed to grow tenuous. A moment later the ground was solid again and, try as I might, I could not recover that sense of mystery that had overwhelmed me just a moment before.

**

Sitting on this ledge tonight I am a scientist, but I am torn by conflicting needs. I need to understand, and my brain is filled with a constant chatter of explaining words. I wait also for God to visit me in the wind, and I watch spirits dance on the surface of the lake far below.

~~

[1] I found these words and the previous words in some notes of mine and I don't remember if they were taken from a lecture or from a textbook. If I have failed to give proper attribution please forgive me. I will certainly correct the error if you know of a reference.

3 MYTH

"That psychologist you mentioned earlier. What was his name?"

I look over to see my friend emptying soup powder into a cup of hot water held by his wife. She stirs it and sips a bit before passing it back to him. It is late afternoon and we have been talking on and off for several hours. This is a layover day for me and I spent it hiking short distances from my camp, eating, reading, and watching shadow and cloud play with the sun. The camp is in a meadow sheltered by two spurs of rock extending outward from a massive cone of mountain to the north. I watched the sunrise from one of these spurs and now sit waiting for sunset. A stream of clear water cascades below my feet, next to a footpath that rises from the pine forest below.

An elderly couple came up that footpath in early afternoon and, after only a few moments of talk, we agreed to share this piece of mountain for the night. They tell me that they are Taos pueblos living in Los Angeles. He is a retired engineer from Lockheed, and wears a black nylon jacket bearing a bright shoulder patch identifying the shuttle mission that placed the Hubble telescope in orbit. A breast insignia shows the telescope itself, solar panels unfurled, shutter open. She is an editor and a poet. One of her volumes is a translation of Taos religious verses into English; it caused a small stir among some anthropologists in the mid-sixties.

"C. G. Jung," I answer his question.

"I knew him," the old engineer reminisces. "He visited my home with a group of Americans when I was a child. He sat with our chief on the roof and they talked all day. I liked him."

His wife brings the cup of soup to her lips to hide her smile. Are they playing a joke on me?

"You were present when Carl Jung met Ochwiay Biano?" I ask incredulously.

∗∗

"Science is not a body of belief, but rather a process by which such beliefs are acquired, modified, and discarded. Most scientists don't realize this, and they spend their lives acting and talking about things as if they were actually true. They do this despite the fact that what scientists believe today is not what scientists believed yesterday, and despite the reasonable assumption that what scientists believe today is not what scientists will believe tomorrow.

"At its deepest core, the beliefs of science change. I personally wonder how much longer the atomic theory will last."

The speaker was a heretic, of course, but he was a friendly heretic and he had earned our respect with a remarkable body of work spanning almost thirty years. I had just discovered the writings of C.G. Jung and was trying to connect Jung's ideas about myth to what this physicist turned molecular biologist was saying about science.

"What we are to our inward vision," Jung had said, "can only be expressed by way of myth. Myth is more individual and expresses life more precisely than does science." [1]

He also said, "Unfortunately, the mythic side of man is given short shrift nowadays. He can no longer create fables. As a result, a great deal escapes him; for it is important and salutary to speak also of incomprehensible things." [2]

Great scientists create great fables, I thought to myself.

**

"Does that surprise you?" my friend asks. His wife's smile becomes wider.

"It is ironic," I answer.

"Why is that?" his wife laughs, enjoying the moment.

**

Ochwiay Biano had been chief of the Taos pueblos when Jung visited and wrote about them in the 1920's. It was Jung's first opportunity to see himself and his culture through the eyes of a radically different mind.

> "We think that they are all mad."
> I asked him why he thought the whites were all mad.
> "They say that they think with their heads," he replied.
> "Why of course. What do you think with?" I asked him in surprise.
> "We think here," he said, indicating his heart. [3]

Jung learned during his visit that Ochwiay Biano was concerned that the American government was trying to suppress his religion. He was worried about this, not only for his own people, but for everyone on the planet.

> "What we do, we do not only for ourselves but for the

Americans also. Yes, we do it for the whole world. Everyone benefits by it. ...

"We are a people who live on the roof of the world; we are the sons of Father Sun, and with our religion we daily help our father to go across the sky. We do this not only for ourselves, but for the whole world. If we were to cease practicing our religion, in ten years the sun would no longer rise. Then it would be night forever." [4]

**

I'm at a loss for words. I look at the Hubble telescope insignia sewn on the black nylon jacket, and I think about the prayers needed to help the Sun across the sky. I want to hold both of these contradictory worlds in my head. Something in me needs to do this, but my ears are roaring and I'm losing it.

"Not there," the woman prods. "You can't hold it there."

And then I feel it. A buzzing heat spirals out from my breastbone into the rest of my body and these contradictory ideas drop from my head into my chest where they unite and become a single thing.

The man is speaking, or perhaps chanting.

"What I believe when I visit my people in my village fills my heart with pride. My prayers help the Sun to move across the sky, and this I gladly do.

"What I believe when I visit my colleagues at the Cape fills my heart with pride. My programs help Hubble look out into space and back into time."

"It is not a contradiction to believe both of these things," the woman intervenes, "because neither of them is true."

And then the laughter begins.

My friends are asleep. It is very dark. I am sitting here on this spur of rock trying to hold these contradictions in my chest. I can't do it, and as they fade the feeling of loss is almost unbearable. In a moment I'll start to cry; I feel the tears even now. It's OK, by morning I won't remember their origins.

~~

[1] C.G. Jung, Memories, Dreams, Reflections (New York, Vintage Books, 1965), 3.

[2] C.G. Jung, Memories, Dreams, Reflections (New York, Vintage Books, 1965), 300.

[3] C.G. Jung, Memories, Dreams, Reflections (New York, Vintage Books, 1965), 248.

[4] C.G. Jung, Memories, Dreams, Reflections (New York, Vintage Books, 1965), 251-252.

4 MIRRORS …

The mountain is in cloud this morning and I wake in a mist that, having deposited a fine layer of dew on the outer skin of my sleeping bag, now stands sentinel in patches throughout the clearing. I brace myself to the cold, dress, and walk stiffly down to the stream to collect water for tea. Beyond the stream I can occasionally make out, framed in the trees, the glassy surface of a nearby lake. Shreds of mist hang above the lake, silent and immobile — bits of frost on an otherwise perfect mirror.

I rinse out my pots in the stream; fill one of them with clean water, and am about to turn back towards camp when I see him. He stands there on the other side of the stream in blue jeans and a Pendleton shirt buttoned high at the neck. One of his shirt pockets contains a pocket protector and three or four pens; a calculator dangles from a nylon case looped through his belt. He watches me from behind horn-rimmed glasses with an open, yearning expression.

I don't want to talk to him, but neither can I just turn my back on him and return to camp.

**

While a graduate student I lived in an on-campus dormitory called the Graduate College. Its bell tower rose above two quadrangles of dark, stone buildings situated at the edge of the university's golf course. Tradition required all students to appear for meals in full baccalaureate gown, and the sight of six hundred intense young men and women moving about the grounds in black robes was quite amusing to outsiders.

The residents of the Graduate College referred to their home as the G.C. So did the undergraduates on the lower campus. For them, however, G.C. was short for Goon Castle.

I didn't like hearing this alternate description of my home, and I was embarrassed for the small colony of socially awkward intellectuals that had earned this reputation for us. I found some of the customs adopted by the males in this group to be especially vexing. They buttoned their shirts high at the neck, and always carried three or four pens in a pocket protector in their left shirt pocket. Many also carried a slide rule in a leather case looped through their belt.

These elements of dress became a badge for me that I used to identify a class of people. If I met a stranger possessing even two of the four elements of this uniform, I felt that I could look into his soul and see all the important features of his life. Caught in a chance encounter, I would often look away. The connection was too intimate.

Years later, at a reunion of students from the university's biology department, someone showed me a picture taken at a department softball game. I was clearly visible at the edge of the group — fondling the slide rule hanging from my belt, shirt buttoned high, pocket protector and pens clearly visible.

**

Behind me in the camp is a copy of Douglas Hofstadter's book *Gödel, Escher, Bach*. The bookmark is positioned at the end of the dialog between Chapters 5 and 6, "Canon by Intervallic Augmentation." [1] In the overview at the beginning of this book there is a description of the dialog which begins:

> Achilles and the Tortoise try to resolve the question, "Which contains more information — a record, or the phonograph which plays it?" [2]

Psychologists rarely have trouble answering this question.

"It's the phonograph," they will almost always say.

A record contains a single, spiraled groove of information encoded in the walls of plastic that form the groove. A phonograph must know that these walls constitute a code which, with the right key, can be decrypted into the atmospheric vibrations that make music. In "Canon by Intervallic Augmentation" the Tortoise tells his friend Achilles about a jukebox owned by his friend the Crab. Unlike most jukeboxes (which consist of a single phonograph and many records), the Crab's jukebox contains a single record and many phonographs. Each phonograph interprets the groove of the single record in a different way, and so the jukebox exhibits a wide range of musical selections.

People are like phonographs. The universe offers humanity a record to play. Different people, however, elicit different music from this record. It's called projection.

Each of us has many attributes, but we acknowledge only a few of them. The rest are unconscious. If we see ourselves as popular we deny our awkwardness. If we see ourselves as weak we deny our strength. But what we deny still exists, and it will find a way to be expressed — if not as part of us, then as part of something else. A single individual, event, or circumstance can stir our unconscious and cause it to "project" itself onto the blank parts of any situation. It feels as if it is "out there", but it really isn't.

I'm reminded of all this as I look across the stream towards my apparition. A tatter of mist on his right dissolves and I discover that he's not alone. Standing there with him is the most beautiful woman that I have ever seen. Her hair falls straight to her shoulders and frames an expressionless face that watches me with what seems to be enormous compassion and understanding. She's dressed in a simple gown, drawn tight at the waist — unadorned, elegant. I am transfixed — her eyes look into me, join me, and invite me to open myself to her.

I begin to speak and I quickly find those deep pools I want most to share. As I speak, her face remains carefully controlled, but I can see from her eyes that she understands what I am trying to say. Of all the women I have known only she can fill the void I feel exposed within me, and I ache for her to step across the stream, to join me, and to share my life.

Tears well up, my vision blurs, I blink my eyes several times. When I look again both man and woman are gone — a mirror stands upright on the other side of the stream; in it I see my own reflection. Slowly the mirror transforms, and I see shreds of mist hanging above the glassy surface of the lake, framed by the trees.

~~

[1] Douglas R. Hofstadter, Godel, Escher, Bach: an Eternal Golden Braid (New York, Basic Books, 1979), 153–157.

[2] Douglas R. Hofstadter, Godel, Escher, Bach: an Eternal Golden Braid (New York, Basic Books, 1979), ix.

5 … AND REFLECTIONS

I've hunched down in a shallow depression, above tree line, on one side of the ridge of rock I have been traversing. There's no time for me to move lower — the thunderheads are only moments away, above and below me, spanning my entire field of view. Flashes of light within massive anvils of cloud precede by less than a second the deep throated rumbles rolled out by the same furnace.

This extraordinary display of power is so real, so imminent, that my mind has simply embraced it — I watch; I wait; I wonder what it will do to me.

**

"Your loss of faith … where is it in your body?"

The psychiatrist sat across from me, facing me. Her voice was very quiet, but also very insistent. We both knew that we were about to enter new territory.

"It isn't in my body at all," I answered. "It's outside, behind my left shoulder."

I had entered this room for the first time just over a year ago. I had come to find some kind of relief for the terrible depression that had engulfed me following the loss of my laboratory. I was forty years old, and I knew that I would never again stand at a bench, move glassware, and puzzle over lists of numbers in a loose-leaf notebook. Together we were trying to find new sources of energy for me in the labyrinthine mental corridors that I was discovering existed behind my eyes.

We had found an especially powerful tool in my attempts to identify within my body the physical locations of emotional energy. The union of powerful but contradictory ideas was always accompanied by a buzzing heat in my breastbone, and the opening of a cavity in my chest. Confrontations with tax collectors and bankers were experienced as sharp, weeklong bouts of intestinal cramps. I came to view these locations as the chakras referred to by Hindu yogis. We had been mapping my "chakras", and the pathways of energy that connected them, for many months. Today, for the first time, we would open one, and peer inside.

"What does it feel like?" the psychiatrist asked.

"It's very tangible," I answered. "It's a physical presence. I can almost feel it with the hairs on the left side of my neck."

"Do you want to bring it around in front, between us, where we can both look at it?" Her voice was impassive — no hint of what she thought was appropriate here.

"Yes," I said.

It resisted. I could get it across my shoulder, and just inside my peripheral vision. Then I would lose control of it, and it would drift back behind me to its apparently natural position. We persisted, however, and after ten minutes of strenuous effort it floated between us, knee high.

"What do you see?" she asked.

"It looks like a hard sphere of black marble," I said. "It's about the size of a bowling ball."

"Anything else?"

"There are fine lines of bright light running through it. They aren't pulsing or moving; they're just steady, continuous, lines of light."

"There's something else," she said.

I watched for several minutes in silence. There was no strain involved in keeping this thing in view, but neither was there anything else to see.

Finally the psychiatrist asked, "What are you looking at."

"The lines of light," I answered.

"Ah," she replied. "Don't look there. Look in the dark places between the lines."

What happened next was instantaneous. For a single moment, an old man looked out at me from within the marble sphere.

"An old man," I exclaimed. "There's an old man in there."

"Who is he?" she asked.

"Moses," I replied.

"You've found him," she said quietly.

**

The storm has arrived. I must hold my parka close to my body to keep it from catching the wind and carrying me away. Lightning strikes repeatedly at the ridge just above, and the rain stings my face with magnificent, cold fury. I feel the thunder as continuous waves of vibration throughout my entire body. Within, I simply wait, and wonder what will happen next.

**

"The unconscious is, by definition, unconscious," the

psychiatrist said. "You can't look inward to find it; rather, it projects itself onto the circumstances of your life. You can't see it, but you must live within the shell of reflections that it sends to you."

"But how do I know what is projection and what is real?" I asked.

"They're both real," she replied.

Moses stayed with me for several months. I tried once or twice to bring him back to the front where I could see him, but my attempts were both half-hearted and unnecessary. We had been introduced; I knew where he was; I could feel him behind me — just over my left shoulder.

I can't describe how he did it, but he healed a small part of me. For the first time since my departure I returned to the campus and walked the corridors of the medical school that had been my home. I stopped by the library to read recent papers in my research area. I even dropped by my old laboratory to visit its new occupant, an old friend. It was very difficult, but my past was now my past and my future was beginning to reveal itself.

One morning I woke to discover that Moses was gone — or rather, that I could no longer feel his presence outside my body. Sometime during the night, in a dream, the black marble sphere had softened into a mist and become a part of my conscious mind. The projection was withdrawn, and my conscious self expanded a tiny bit to include part of its source.

**

The air is clean and smells of ozone. Massive, dark clouds move quickly but silently past me to follow the now departed storm. I am sitting on a broad, flat boulder on the ridge and can look both up at a sky that is beginning to show patches of blue, and down on either side into canyons of cloud, of very green forests and very blue lakes. There are many lakes, and they are interconnected by numerous mountain streams. Their shining reminds me of Indra's Net.

> The Buddhist allegory of "Indra's Net" tells of an endless net of threads throughout the universe, the horizontal threads running through space, the vertical ones through time. At every crossing of threads is an individual, and every individual is a crystal bead. The great light of "Absolute Being" illuminates and penetrates every crystal bead: moreover, every crystal bead reflects not only the light from every other crystal in the net — but also every reflection of every reflection throughout the universe. [1]

**

The years following my introduction to Moses have led me to realize that an enormous amount of the world in which I live is generated by me. The line between what's "in here" and what's "out there" has become increasingly difficult to define. Why this should be accompanied by a sense of greater sanity rather than less, I can't say. I know only that the universe appears to me as a great house of mirrors populated by reflections of reflections of reflections. Where it ends ... if it ends ... I no longer know.

Why Moses? My journeys towards sanity are also journeys towards God; the symbols of my healing are always symbols of religious experience. In some ways I think this must be true for everyone.

Have you ever wondered, for example, how some of our ancestors stumbled upon the gods of Mount Olympus? It seems to me now that those gods were (are?) simply projections of those strong emotions we are unable to own ourselves. It is easier to be possessed by rage than to feel it as an integral part of our own souls. This thought first occurred to me on reading Marion Zimmer Bradley's account of the Trojan Wars.

> ... Despite the well-known form and the features now clearly visible in the moonlight, this was not her husband. How this could be she did not know, but around his shoulders a flicker of errant lightning seemed to play, and as he walked his foot struck the flagstones with the faintest sound of faraway thunder. He seemed to have grown taller, his head thrown back against the levin-light which crackled in his hair. Leda knew, with a shudder that bristled down the small hairs of her body, that one of the stranger Gods was now abroad within the semblance of her husband, riding him as he would mount and ride one of his own horses. The lightning-flare told her it was Olympian Zeus, controller of thunders, Lord of Lightning.
> This was nothing new to her; she knew the feel of the Goddess filling and overflowing her body when she blessed the harvests or when she lay in the fields drawing down the Divine power of growth to the grain. She remembered how she seemed to stand aside from her familiar self, and it was the Goddess who moved through the rites, dominating everyone else with the power within Her.[2]

And other Gods? If we withdraw the projections of our own emotions, and accept ownership of them, what next comes to the surface? Jehovah? Christ? Silence?

Is it possible to withdraw all projections and become fully conscious? Not, I suspect, if we are to remain human. We are beings partitioned between consciousness and unconsciousness, and we live in the house of mirrors built where they meet. In this house, if we choose to look, perhaps we find God.

John Freeman interviewed Carl Jung in 1959 for the BBC television program "Face to Face."

What sort of religious upbringing did your father give you?

Oh, we were Swiss Reformed.

And did he make you attend church regularly?

Oh, well, that was quite natural. Everyone went to church on Sunday.

And did you believe in God?

Oh, yes.

Do you now believe in God?

Now? [Pause.] Difficult to answer. I know. I don't need to believe. I know. [3]

Freud first gave the unconscious a name over a century ago. I can't conceive of what it must be like to live without an awareness of its presence. And yet, fifteen years ago, it was only a word to me — no closer as an experience than the surface of Mars.

~~

[1] Douglas R. Hofstadter, Godel, Escher, Bach: an Eternal Golden Braid (New York, Basic Books, 1979), 258.

[2] Marion Zimmer Bradley, Firebrand (New York, Simon and Schuster, 1987), 18–19.

[3] William McGuire and R.F.C. Hull, C.G. Jung Speaking: Interviews and Encounters (Princeton, Princeton University Press, 1977), 427–428.

6 EYES

I've been traveling cross country for almost three days, away from the well-marked trails. My days are filled with the sounds of buzzing insects, wind, and the purling of the stream that I have been following. I have neither visitors nor visions as companions. The world seems quite ordinary. Have I withdrawn my projections from the world, or have I simply replaced them with projections of a different, more commonplace, variety.

There's no way to know, of course. We all live within our own, very unique, brains. We are bathed in experiences that come to us along neural pathways from places we can never visit. I can't reach out and touch the water of this stream next to me. I can only experience the hallucination of such a touch — sent to me by my body as it does unknowable things.

**

The cat lay prone in a support harness that kept its head immobile. The muscles attached to its eyes were also immobile and so the cat looked fixedly at one spot on the far wall where images played on a simple, white screen. As light from the screen entered the lens in the cat's eye, it was focused on the retina in the back of the eyeball where it formed a miniature, inverted replica of the scene playing out before it.

The retina is a mosaic of tiny cells called photoreceptors that respond to light by dispatching electrical signals into webs of living fibers that form circuits in the back wall of the eye. When an image is focused on the retina some of these photoreceptors are bathed in light and send signals into the web; others remain silently in shadow.

Deep in the web are other cells, the retinal ganglion cells, which participate in the calculations of the web and then send the results further into the cat's brain along a thick cable of fibers called the optic nerve. The information is received by two knee-shaped bundles of nerve cells called the lateral geniculate nuclei which perform additional calculations and then send their results along the optic radiation to the surface of the rear of the brain, the primary visual cortex.

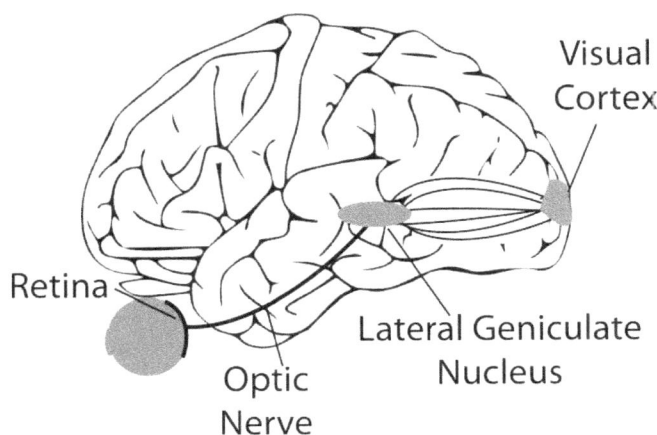

The students gathered around this cat were studying how cats (and, presumably, people) calculate and transmit vision information. At this moment they were listening to the signals leaving a single retinal ganglion cell and entering the optic nerve — a single pop in the speaker on the wall every time the ganglion cell fired. As a single spot of light traced a search pattern of descending, horizontal lines on the screen before the cat, the speaker emitted a modest background of pops. Suddenly the popping sounds from the speaker increased in frequency.

"That's it," said the professor near the projector that controlled the spot of light on the screen. She reversed the motion of the spot of light and narrowed her search pattern to this smaller region of the screen — stopping periodically. A student stood at the screen with a felt-tipped pen. Each time the spot of light stopped he would listen to the sound from the speaker. If the pops sounded at "normal" background frequency, he did nothing; if the pops increased in frequency he marked a small "x" on the screen; if the pops decreased in frequency he marked the screen with a triangle.

A pattern quickly emerged.

```
         Δ  Δ  Δ
       Δ  Δ
     Λ        Δ  Δ
        x x x      Δ
   Δ    x
        x   x   x  Δ
   Δ     x
     Δ    x     x  Δ
       Δ    Δ
       Δ      Δ   Δ
            Δ
```

"This is the classic response pattern of an 'on-center cell'," the professor said. "The region encompassed by both x's and triangles is called its receptive field. Notice that if I increase the size of the light spot to encompass the entire receptive field, the firing rate of the ganglion cell doesn't change very much as I turn the light on and off. To get a response from this cell I must illumine at least part of its center while keeping its periphery in shadow (to increase firing rate), or illumine its periphery while keeping its center in shadow (to decrease firing rate).

"Each ganglion cell in the retina receives input from many photoreceptors. It performs calculations on these inputs and then sends information about lighting contrasts to its target in the lateral geniculate nucleus.

"You might think it would be simpler if ganglion cells just fired at a rate proportional to the light shining on its region of retina — a video camera that sends its signal back to the control room for interpretation." She paused. "But this is the control room. Pattern interpretation begins even before the message leaves the eye!"

By the end of the afternoon the students had found cells in the cat's visual pathway that dealt with quite abstract classes of pattern — retinal ganglion cells that responded only to large moving objects; cells in the primary visual cortex that only responded to light-dark edges that moved from left to right.

"The picture that gets to where this cat lives is not a picture at all," the professor summarized. "Rather, it's a location and a list of properties. ... 'Attention, zone 5132 reports that a vertical dark edge is moving across its field of view.'"

"But that's not what I see," complained a student. "I look at you and I see you, not a list of abstract shape classifications."

"That's because you have a very good imagination," smiled the professor. "You're visual system whispers you a story, and you manufacture a quite compelling movie to replace it." [1]

**

The stream quits the forest to cut across a high alpine meadow. Without trees to block my view, I can see forever.

"Who's out there?" I ask. The stream is amused; it laughs.

**

I have spent my life listening to whispered stories. I have created a universe out of those stories, and I live in it. But where am I really?

Wherever I am, it seems as if there are others here with me. We talk to each other about where we are and we agree on certain features. There are other things that only I can see. Are they less real?

Most of my apparent companions believe that reality consists only of those experiences that we all share in common. I don't know, but it is my myth that I am living in a vivid, three-dimensional map. In this myth the features of this map that I share with my apparent companions are "out there." The features that are unique to me are "in here." It is also my myth that the difference between "in here" and "out there" is not as apparent as it might seem.

C.G. Jung devoted an important part of his professional life to interpreting the writings of alchemists. You may know that alchemists sought after a "philosopher's stone" that turned lead into gold by manipulating and combining ordinary materials in special ways. You may not know, however, that the gold sought was a spiritual rather than a material gold, and the process of achieving the philosopher's stone was psychological rather than physical.

Take of common rainwater a good quantity, at least ten quarts, preserve it well sealed in glass vessels for at least ten days, then it will deposit matter and faeces on the bottom. Pour off the clear liquid and place in a wooden vessel that is fashioned round like a ball, cut it through the middle and fill the vessel a third full, and set it in the sun about midday in a secret or secluded spot.

When this has been done, take a drop of the consecrated red wine and let it fall into the water, and you will instantly perceive a fog and thick darkness on top of the water, such as also was at the first creation. Then put in two drops, and you will see the light coming forth from the darkness; whereupon little by little put in every half of each quarter hour first three, then four, then five, then six drops, and then no more, and you will see with your own eyes one thing after another appearing by and by on top of the water, how God created all things in six days, and how it all came to pass, and such secrets as are not to be spoken aloud and I also have not the power to reveal. Fall on your knees before you undertake this operation. Let your eyes judge of it; for thus was the world created. Let all stand as it is, and in half an hour after it began it will disappear.

By this you will see clearly the secrets of God, that are at present hidden from you as from a child. You will understand what Moses has written concerning the creation; you will see what manner of body Adam and Eve had before and after the Fall, what the serpent was, what the tree, and what manner of fruits they ate: where and what Paradise is, and in what bodies the righteous shall be resurrected; not in this body that we have received from Adam, but in that which we attain through the Holy Ghost, namely in such a body as our Saviour brought from heaven. [2]

Jung comments:

The alchemical opus deals in the main not just with chemical experiments as such, but with something resembling psychic processes expressed in pseudochemical language. The ancients knew more or less what chemical processes were; therefore they must have known that the thing they practiced was, to say the least of it, no ordinary chemistry. ...

In seeking to explore [the real nature of matter] he projected the unconscious into the darkness of matter in order to illuminate it. In order to explain the mystery of matter he projected yet another mystery — his own unknown psychic background — into what was to be explained: Obscurum per obscurius, ignotum per ignotius! This procedure was not, of course, intentional; it was an involuntary occurrence.[3]

I have wondered at these alchemists who unknowingly devoted their lives to reading ink blots, but I realize that I am no different. I sit somewhere inside my neural network and build stories out of the stuff that is sent my way. Some of this stuff comes from mythic places with names like "optic radiation" or "auditory nerve." Other parts of this stuff come from equally mythic but more plastic places that I call my unconscious. All of it is assembled into a seamless whole long before I experience it.

**

The broad vistas of this meadow have once again given way to forest. Through the trees I see a well kept path that leads to a clearing and a small chapel. Although this part of the mountain is far from any of the marked hiking trails, I am not surprised.

I'm sure it will be an interesting visit.

~~

[1] An excellent discussion of signal processing in the visual system can be found in Eric R. Kandel and James H. Schwartz, Principles of Neural Science, 2nd Edition (Elsevier, New York, 1985), 366–383.

[2] C.G. Jung, Psychology and Alchemy (Princeton, Princeton University Press, 1980), 246.

[3] C.G. Jung, Psychology and Alchemy (Princeton, Princeton University Press, 1980), 244–5.

7 FIRST LESSONS

"I'm having trouble putting all of this together," I say to the couple behind me.

"Us too," they laugh.

We're standing in a shallow basin of rock above permanent snow fields — the entire sky open to us on a cloudless, windless night. In the Southwest I see Sagittarius approach the horizon; Uranus and Neptune should be nearby, but I don't see them. In the East a waning, gibbous moon has risen with Aries. Mars is there too, faintly visible in the scatter of moonlight.

Half an hour ago I awoke from a dream in which I was riding a space shuttle in orbit with two friends — an elderly couple I had met on a camping trip. We were standing in the large cargo bay looking out at the five stars of the Southern Cross when the man turned to me and said, "I've never seen these stars before."

"You still haven't," I answered. "This is a dream."

Instantly, the sensations of the shuttle became uncommonly vivid.

"I am dreaming," I exclaimed as the sights, sounds, smells, and touch of the spacecraft became increasingly real. I tried to move my arm and awoke instead in my sleeping bag, breathing chill night air and looking up into a magnificent sky. The woman was sitting near me on a low boulder; her husband stood farther away — watching the night sky.

"So you want to see mysteries," she laughed. "Time to start school."

**

"I have something to show you," our host smiled.

I was in a small Cambridge apartment — one of many guests gathered for friendship. Our host was standing on a chair in the middle of the room and checking the connections of wires that laced both ceiling and walls. Tiny, colored glass beads were spaced evenly along the wires; they looked like Christmas tree lights.

"Ready," he announced to his wife who was standing by the light switch at the door.

The lights went out and, for almost a minute, we were in total darkness. Harpsichord music began to play from speakers placed in each of the four corners of the room — a Bach fugue — and the room was filled with tiny points of flickering light. The lights danced in perfect harmony with the music; the patterns of notes and the patterns of light wove an intricate web of sensation that transported me into a weightless night of singing stars.

When the music ended it took me several moments to remember where I was, and to feel the loss.

"A computer?" asked a physician from the medical school.

"You might say that," said our host.

The physician walked over the stereo console and examined it.

"Where is it?" he asked.

"In your head," our host laughed. "The lights flicker at random; your mind seeks a pattern to match the music."

**

"What do you see?" the woman asks.

"Planets, stars, galaxies," I answer.

"No," she feigns anger. "I don't want to know what you're thinking. I want to know what you're seeing."

"I'm a scientist. I look at this sky and visualize a clockwork mechanism of orbiting planets, stars, and galaxies.

Silence.

I'm suddenly embarrassed, even ashamed. I don't want to tell this woman what I really see.

**

My mother gave me a telescope when I was twelve. North of our house was a corn field that stretched back from the highway into a dark Wisconsin night. Early in summer, before the corn was too high, I could place a card table in that field, a mount for my small refractor, and seek the planets. Venus, Mars, and Jupiter were easy, but Saturn eluded me. A trip to the library uncovered a book that told me where to look; this same book also introduced me to the ecliptic.

Most of the sky consists of fixed points of light, distant stars that never move with respect to one another — at least in a single lifetime. As the Earth rotates beneath them they move across the sky in a fixed order and the constellations never change. A narrow band of sky running roughly East-West, however, is filled with lights that move against the stars — the Sun, the Moon, the planets. One of the great intellectual feats of my life was to hold a picture of the night sky (as seen from Wisconsin) and a picture of the solar system (with its central sun and orbiting planets) simultaneously in mind and to see the relationship between them.

All of the planets of the solar system orbit about the Sun in roughly the same plane.

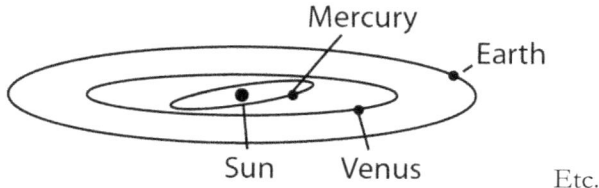

Imagine that you're standing on the Earth and looking out into the sky above or below that plane. No planets move there; the sky is fixed. Now bring your gaze down into the plane occupied by the planets; now, suddenly, things change on a nightly basis. This narrow band of transience is called the ecliptic and the twelve constellations of distant stars that lie in this band are the constellations of the Zodiac — Cancer, Leo, Virgo, Libra, Scorpius, Sagittarius, Capricornus, Aquarius, Pisces, Aries, Taurus, and Gemini.

These are, of course, also the symbols and relationships used by astrologers to map human events and, at twelve; I could not separate the disciplines of astronomy and astrology.

My explorations of the heavens from my card table in the middle of a Wisconsin corn field became a matter of cosmic importance. I was an apprentice astrologer and I was learning the skills required to map humanity's future … and my own.

**

"I see myself," I answer the woman. "I know it can't possibly be true, but I see my own future up there. As the planets move they reveal both opportunities and dangers. It really seems to work!"

The woman says nothing. A bright moon illumines the snow fields that separate us from the broad canyon of pine through which I had approached this place. I see a hawk far below, perhaps searching for food.

**

Every Christmas a few of the students of the Graduate College would hold a "beach party" in one of the sand traps of the university's golf course. One year I remember sitting next to an unusually gifted physics student who often sought out secluded places along the shore of a nearby lake to sit, utterly still in full lotus position, for hours at a time.

"I'm giving it up," he said to me.

"It?" I asked.

"Meditation. I've stopped meditating."

I didn't really know about meditation in those days, and I certainly didn't grasp what he was trying to tell me; but the expression on his face was full of need, and I knew something important had happened to him.

I turned to him and gave him my full attention.

"These last few months I've begun to experience things I can't describe. I've been standing at the edge of a place that is so still, so empty, so compelling, that I know if I go further I won't come back.

"If I could take my physics with me, I'd go; but I don't know if that's possible."

I didn't know what to say.

"Dave," he said, "Last night I flew. Now I have to choose. I'm not big enough to include them both. Am I?"

I still didn't know what to say.

His expression turned sad.

"I thought you'd understand," he finished. "Forgive my ramblings."

**

"Are you afraid of appearing superstitious?" asks the man, joining us.

"He's afraid of going crazy," the woman answers for me. "If he starts believing in astrology; next thing he'll be hearing voices."

"I'm already hearing voices," I say nervously.

**

I met him while walking along Santa Monica Boulevard late on a Thursday evening. He called to me from the shadows of the deeply inset entrance to a large office building.

"Should we reflag the Kuwaiti oil tankers?" he asked. It was during the Iran-Iraq War, and this was an important topic of the day.

I walked into the shadows and sat down on a low wall enclosing carefully manicured shrubbery. His shopping cart contained crushed aluminum cans, some rags, a change of clothes, two books, three cans of beer, and a portable radio. He'd been on the streets a long time — the back of his hands and neck were black with soot. His left arm was in a makeshift sling. He smelled.

"I don't know," I answered. "What do you think?"

He handed me a beer and said in a slow, clear voice, "It sets an impossible precedent. We use Kuwait to manipulate the price of oil, and ..."

It took me only a few minutes to realize that, in his eyes, we weren't alone. His eyes kept darting towards things I couldn't see. His face kept changing — sometimes I saw fear, other times relief.

In the several hours that followed I learned about the economics of Persian Gulf oil, and that his ex-wife and children still lived in the large house in Encino that he and his wife had jointly funded from the earnings of his accounting practice and her law firm.

"That's before I went crazy," he said sadly. "Or maybe it's just the booze."

"You see and hear things that aren't there?" I ventured.

"Oh, they're there," he exclaimed. "It's you who can't see them."

"Who are they?" I asked.

"All sorts. Some good, some bad. There are demons, you know! And angels!! They're telling me about you right now, and they want you to know it's going to work out all right."

Something hard stuck in my throat.

"What ..."

"You'll see," he said very seriously. "People like me know about these things. We're closer to God, because we need so much more help."

He stood up and put his hands on my shoulders — the smell of beer, sweat, and urine was almost unbearable.

"Lord? You there? Help my friend here! He needs to understand what's happening."

He retreated to his shopping cart, suddenly shy, and said, "It'll be OK now. It may take a while, but you'll see."

I felt a desperate need to leave this place. I stood up and began to back away.

"Can I help you?" I asked.

"I could use a few bucks," he answered.

I gave him ten dollars, and told him that maybe things would get better. It sounded hypocritical.

"You never know," he said.

Leaving the shadows I re-entered the brightly lit boulevard. I heard him call to a young couple waiting at the street light. They turned around, saw me, and then looked into the shadows behind me. I walked swiftly away.

**

"You're afraid of becoming like him?" asks the woman.

I hesitate.

"Yes," I answer.

"If it happens it won't be because of your visions," she whispers. "It's not that you see; it's what you see and what you do with what you see. Some people are torn apart; others are put together."

"That's tonight's lesson," the man interjects. "Visions don't make you crazy. Visions just make you change."

**

"Did you ever see The Exorcist?" my friend asked.

We were sitting in a restaurant on a lazy Saturday afternoon.

"Yes," I answered.

"Do you remember the scene where the old priest is standing in the night at the door of the possessed girl's house … waiting to enter."

"Yes."

"I've been having dreams where I'm in that house, and I know that such a figure is waiting for me at the door. But the figure isn't a priest. It's evil!

"Each time I have the dream the figure is closer to my bedroom. Outside the front door. Inside the front door. Up the stairs. Outside my bedroom. Inside my bedroom — sitting in a chair in a shadowed corner.

"Three nights ago it was so real I hid under the sheets. I couldn't look!"

"I've had dreams like that," I mused. "I think you have to look."

"I did, finally," he smiled. "Last night. ... I threw back the covers and turned the lights on so that I could look at it squarely. ... You'll never guess what I saw."

I remained silent.

"It was me!" he laughed. "I was sitting in the corner. ... I don't think I'll have the dream again."

**

Leo has risen above the Eastern horizon, but it will soon fade with dawn. A gentle but bitingly cold wind has appeared out of the North. The couple has departed, but I feel the presence of many old friends that have gathered with me for the sun's rising. A priest has climbed up here from Jerusalem to speak with the wind; a physicist sits silently in full lotus at the edge of the snow line; an Indian is preparing the rituals that will assure the continued rising of the sun.

A man stands next to me, keeping an unsteady balance with the frame of a shopping cart. He hands me a warm beer. I feel broken into a thousand pieces by a life I cannot begin to understand. But I also feel myself coming slowly together — one tiny fragment at a time.

8 MIND

"Why would you want one?" The words emerge from an hour's silence.

"One what?" I ask.

"An unconscious," she responds.

We're lying, belly down, on a flat sheet of warm rock, watching the waders in the hot springs. A poorly maintained dirt road winds its way to this site from a two-lane highway five miles to the East and terminates in a nearby dusty field that serves as parking lot for five four-wheel-drive vehicles and a single, vintage, Volkswagen bug.

She owns the bug. She's about to leave her summer job with the forest service to return to graduate studies in entomology at UC Berkeley. I met her in the last mile of my hike down from the sharp spires of volcanic rock that form our mutual, western horizon. I'm certain that I've met her before, perhaps in a mirror, but she doesn't recall it.

"Sometimes it gives me answers," I say.

"Me too. I do my best thinking when I'm not thinking."

**

"Aspartyl transcarbamylase is a well-studied example of

44

an enzyme exhibiting positive cooperativity. Early experiments …" the professor halted in mid-sentence, put down his chalk and turned to examine us. His face had a quizzical expression — as if he didn't know the reason for his pause. His next words were hesitant.

"It's time you learned something," he said. "There are two kinds of science — public science and private science. Public science is what you say when you report a discovery. Private science is what really happened."

I was instantly alert. I knew what he was going to say; I had heard it before.

My last year of high school was hallmarked by senior English. My teacher was famous for her classes on Shakespeare, especially Macbeth. She was also the only teacher in the school qualified to teach both English and mathematics, and she sometimes used her classes to teach both.

One day we explored "solving problems." The blackboard was strewn with a long list of student-suggested tools for problem solving. We had carefully appreciated each one, and there were only five minutes left in the hour.

"All of these tools are marvelous," she said, "and they will keep you out of a heap of trouble if you remember them.

"There is, however, one other method you should know about. I don't know how it works, and you can't command its presence on all occasions. Some people, in fact, never learn how to use it. But who knows, you might get lucky."

While working towards her master's degree in mathematics several decades earlier she had come upon a problem she couldn't solve. Perhaps you remember problems in the calculus where you must find the volume of a space enclosed by intersecting, curved lines rotated about a maliciously chosen axis. She had been working on the problem for the better part of the afternoon but could not picture the volume in her mind. Consequently, she was unable to select a path to transform her initial set of equations into an expression that would give her an answer.

Late in the evening, exhausted, she fell into a fitful sleep in which she was chased by an unusually ugly monster. She awoke when she realized that her monster was a geometric figure with the shape she was seeking.

My biochemistry professor was repeating the same lesson. "… Kekule was unable to find a structure for benzene that explained its hydrogen content. He reports that the answer came to him in a dream in which he saw six snakes arranged in a circle — tail to mouth. The hydrogen content is explained if benzene has a circular structure!"

**

"This forest also thinks by not thinking," she muses.

The day is drawing into late afternoon and this valley is in shadow. The air is cool but our rock remains comfortably warm — perpetually heated by the collaboration of steam and molten rock beneath the hot springs.

"Tell me what you mean," I look over at her.

"Have you ever noticed how the animal trails in the back country maintain themselves? There are no trail crews to clear boulders, repair erosion damage, or plan drainage channels; but they just keep adjusting to conditions, even changing routes when necessary, without any support from the forest service. Storms that devastate man-made trails almost seem to carve new features into natural trails — supporting them, refining them.

"I'm not trying to be mystical. Lots of trails get started and then disappear, but others just keep getting more serviceable over decades, maybe even centuries."

"Maybe the forest has an unconscious," I suggest.

**

I remember clearly the first time that it happened. I was thirteen years old and taking Algebra I. I had been waiting, dreaming, of this moment for almost a year. For me, algebra conjured up images of magicians and sorcerers who spoke of Deep Secrets with expressions like $y = 2x$. I had no idea how y could equal 2x (I didn't really know what y and x were!) but I believed that the Secrets of the Universe were contained in such expressions.

One day my teacher mentioned parenthetically that a point (x, y) and a radius r uniquely defined a circle. That simply meant that if x, y, and r were assigned numeric values, there was one and only one circle that met those conditions.

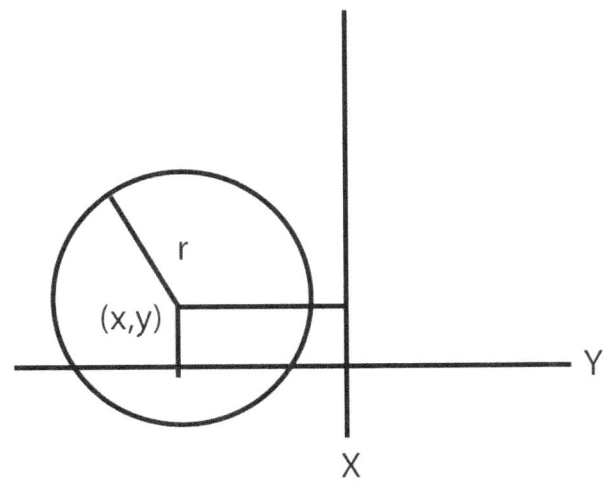

She demonstrated this quite convincingly by tying one end of a piece of string to a thumbtack and the other end to a pencil. She pushed the thumb tack through blank paper on the bulletin board and drew a circle with the string taut. She challenged us to draw a different circle at the same location with the same taut string.

Algebra was the last class of the day and I played with the tack, string, and pencil for a few moments before leaving. I drew a small arc of a circle on the paper.

"What if I draw an arc and then throw away the tack, string, and pencil. How do I find the center again?" I asked.

My teacher was in a hurry to leave and probably didn't really hear my question.

"You can't," she answered from the hallway.

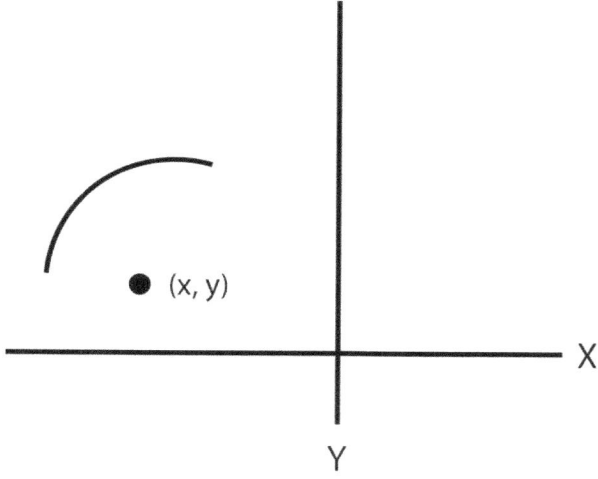

That just didn't make sense to me, but I lacked the tools to study the problem formally. I tried to put the problem aside, but algebra and geometry contained the Secrets of the Universe, and this was my first lesson in alchemy. Every time I closed my eyes I would see an arc, a point, and a line floating in space and I would try to piece them together like a jigsaw puzzle — trying to find the center of the circle. Although my intuition told me that this arc belonged to only one circle with one center I couldn't make the pieces come together as an answer.

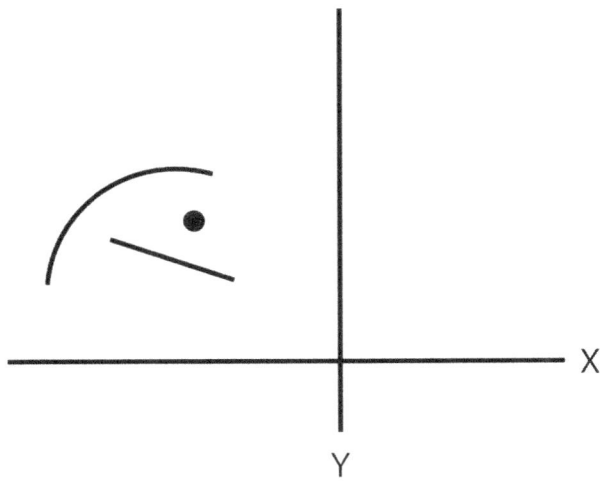

These shapes danced in front of my eyes for almost a week before I began to notice that the line "seemed better" if it lined up with the arc in a "special way." I wanted to say that they were "perpendicular" to each other, but that wasn't right because only two straight lines can be perpendicular to each other. Nevertheless, it seemed to me that if the line was "perpendicular" to the arc (in some loose, metaphorical sense) then the line, if extended, passed through the center of the circle of which the arc was a part.

Perpendicular   Not perpendicular
(in some sense)   (in some sense)

The fact that I knew I was seeing something that I

couldn't express in words made me feel very anxious — my face itched, my chest hurt.

My brain continued to throw random images at me, day after day. Some of them "felt right" and reappeared in slightly different visages. Others "felt wrong" and appeared once or twice only. One day I noticed that my straight line had developed a perpendicular crosspiece, and I noticed that the line was "perpendicular" to the arc only when the crosspiece divided the enclosed area equally.

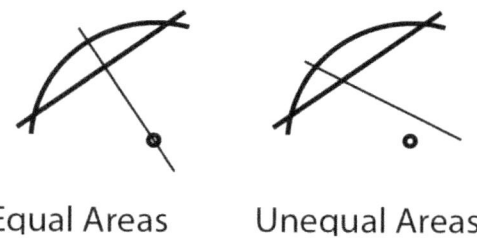

Equal Areas   Unequal Areas

Once I saw the "equal areas" relationship, I became excited. I had a way to describe in words what had been only an aesthetic sense. Furthermore, these dancing shapes had brought me to a place where my conscious mind could take over — I knew how to build such shapes: If a straight line is drawn so as to intersect a circle at two points, the intersection points A and B can be used to draw arcs that define a perpendicular line that bisects AB.

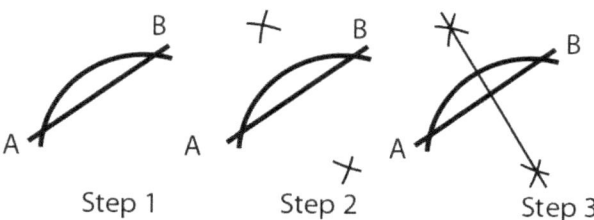

Step 1   Step 2   Step 3

Furthermore, repeating the operation with a second intersecting line A´B´ generated a second perpendicular that specified the center uniquely.

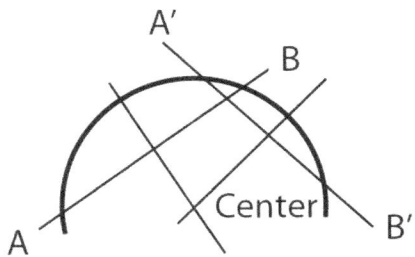

Finding the center

At thirteen I didn't go the next step and "prove" my discovery, but I was pleased nevertheless. I remained excited even after I learned that my discovery was common knowledge to fifteen-year-olds taking geometry. I had journeyed into the unknown alone, and I had come back with new knowledge.

**

"Maybe Statistically Emergent Mentality supersedes the Boolean Dream," she elaborates.

The sun is setting and the air is quite cool. Upwellings of thermal energy keep this rock warm. The others have left the hot springs, and we're alone with this valley's wild creatures. I can see an owl waiting silently on a nearby branch. Mice beware!

**

Eighteenth century England was inhabited by a moth with speckled wings of light color. They lived in trees with a light bark that was encrusted with white lichens. The offspring of these moths always included a few with darker wings, but they stood out against the light background and were easy targets for hungry birds. Few dark colored moths ever survived to reproduce.

The industrial revolution of the nineteenth century brought smoke and soot to England — the lichen died and tree bark grew darker. Suddenly it was the light colored moths that became food for birds and, in only a few decades, England was inhabited by moths with dark wings.

In _On the Origin of Species_ Charles Darwin makes a compelling case for order arising out of random activity. [1] Living creatures reproduce themselves at rates that far outstrip Nature's resources to support them. Each new living creature is also slightly different from its predecessors. Most offspring will die before they ever reproduce. Think of an enormous, buzzing cloud of living creatures each of which is unique. They mate with each other and produce offspring that are equally unique; it is upon this cloud of diversity that natural selection exerts its pressure and new species arise.

It is my myth that ideas arise in a similar fashion. Concepts must reproduce, change, and compete to survive the wilderness of my mind:

• My sensory system sends signals into my neural net and stimulates images — a leaf, a stream, a blue sky.

• These images rapidly multiply into a cloud of similar and diverse images that can be crazy or sane or useful or stupid or anything. These images are also "sticky" and they combine with other images to form larger images that stick together, replicate, stick together again until they form a soup of images, ideas, concepts — "patterns of thought" most of which are utterly irrelevant to my life. They compete below my consciousness as predators and prey; their lives are usually very brief.

• Occasionally the survivors will surface to my awareness — in dreams, in projections.

• Rarely such survivors will remain in my awareness — to become a part of my conscious view of the universe.

**

The owl leaves the tree and we watch it glide silently over the springs and into the field beyond. We lose its flight in shadows.

"Boolean Dream?" I ask.

"I've heard it called that at Berkeley. It refers to computer programs that mimic human thought using rule based systems — no unconscious components allowed."

We see the owl on its flight back to its tree branch. Something struggles in its talons.

**

At any waking moment the human head is filled alive with molecules of thought called notions. The mind is made up of dense clouds of these structures, flowing at random from place to place, bumping against each other and caroming away to bump again, leaving random, two-step tracks like the paths of Brownian motion. They are small round structures, featureless except for tiny projections that are made to fit and then lock onto certain other particles of thought possessing similar receptors. Much of the time nothing comes of the activity. The probability that one notion will encounter a matched one, fitting closely enough for docking, is at the outset vanishingly small.

But when the mind is heated up a little, the movement speeds up and there are more encounters.

The probability is raised.

The receptors are branched and complex, with configurations that are wildly variable. For one notion to fit with another it is not required that the inner structure of either member be the same; it is only the outside signal that counts for docking. But when any two are locked together they become a very small memory. Their motion changes. Now, instead of drifting at random through the corridors of the mind, they move in straight lines, turning over and over, searching for other pairs. Docking and locking continue, pairs are coupled to pairs, and aggregates are formed. These have the look of live, purposeful organisms, hunting for new things to fit with, sniffing for matched receptors, turning things over, catching at everything. As they grow in size, anything that seems to fit, even loosely, is tried on, stuck on, hung from the surface wherever there is room. They become like sea-creatures, decorated all over with other creatures as living symbionts.

At this stage in its development, each mass of conjoined, separate notions, remembering and searching at the same time, shifts into its own fixed orbit, swinging into long elliptical loops around the center of the mind, rotating slowly as it goes. Now it is an idea. [2]

Hofstadter comments:

In other words, subcognition at the bottom will drive cognition at the top. And, perhaps, most importantly, the activities that take place at that top level will neither have been written nor anticipated by any programmer. This is the essence of what I call statistically emergent mentality.

Statistically Emergent Mentality
Supersedes the Boolean Dream [3]

**

This rock is warm enough to ward off the chill and so we haven't unstuffed our sleeping bags. I put away the book I've been reading — it's words curiously relevant to our musings:

A fly was crawling along Saint Liebowitz' nose. The eyes of the saint seemed to be looking cross-eyed at the fly, urging the abbot to brush it away. The abbot had grown fond of the twenty-sixth century wood carving; its face wore a curious smile of a sort that made it rather unusual as a sacramental image. The smile was turned down at one corner; the eyebrows were pulled low in a faintly dubious frown, although there were laugh-wrinkles at the corners of the eyes. Because of the hangman's rope over one shoulder, the saint's expression often seemed puzzling. ...

That little grin will ruin you some day, he warned the image. ... Someday another grim dog will sit in this chair. Cave canem. He'll replace you with a plaster Leibowitz. Long-suffering. One who doesn't look cross-eyed at flies. Then you'll be eaten by termites down in the storage room. To survive the Church's slow sifting of the arts, you have to have a surface that can please a righteous simpleton; and yet you need a depth beneath that surface to please a discerning sage. The sifting is slow, but it gets a turn of the sifter-handle now and then — when some new prelate inspects his episcopal chambers and mutters, "Some of this garbage has got to go." The sifter was usually full of dulcet pap. When the old pap was ground down, fresh pap was added. But what was not ground out was gold, and it lasted. If a church endured five centuries of priestly bad taste, occasional good taste had, by then, stripped away most of the transient tripe, had made it a place of majesty ... [4]

The owl begins another trip into the fields beyond the hot springs. I listen to the sounds of the surrounding forest; will I hear these same sounds in my dreams?

~~

[1] C. Darwin, On the Origin of Species by Means of Natural Selection or the Preservation of Favored Races in the Struggle for Life (London, Murray, 1859).

[2] From Lewis Thomas, in his book The Medusa and the Snail. Quoted in D. R. Hofstadter, Metamagical Themas: Questing for the Essence of Mind and Pattern

(New York, Basic books, 1985), 656.

[3] D. R. Hofstadter, Metamagical Themas: Questing for the Essence of Mind and Pattern (New York, Basic books, 1985), 654.

[4] Walter M. Miller, Jr., A Canticle for Liebowitz (New York, Bantam Books, 1961), 125–126.

9 HARDWARE

Outside my tent the water forms pools in the uneven ground. The rain starts again, and two drops strike the water. Waves expand outward in concentric rings; I wait for them to meet.

**

"You can't patent an idea," he said. "Patent law protects machines, devices, things."

"But computers are universal machines," I protested. "Does it matter that the machine is crafted in software instead of metal?"

> This special property of digital computers, that they can mimic any discrete machine, is described by saying that they are universal machines. The existence of machines with this property has the important consequence that, considerations of speed apart, it is unnecessary to design various new machines to do various computing processes. They can all be done with one digital computer, suitably programmed for each case. It will be seen that as a consequence of this all digital computers are in a sense equivalent. [1]

"Let me give you an example," he answered. "Suppose a

company holds a patent on the design of a cam shaft that, as it turns, opens and closes switches in a specific order at a specific time. Imagine that the ingenuity of this device lies in the precise ordering and timing of the switching.

"In this case, the company's research and development efforts are protected by patent law. Similar devices may not be manufactured and sold without the permission of the company that holds the patent."

"So far so good," I said.

"Right," he answered. "Now suppose that this company replaces its cam shaft with a microcomputer chip that is programmed to open and close switches in the exact same order and time. The invention is no longer a piece of metal with a unique shape; the invention is now a few lines of programming code.

```
If time equals foo then open switch A

Else if time equals foobar then open switch C and
close switch G

Else if ...
```

"So now what does the company own? A machine? A poem? Does legal protection for this property reside in patent law or copyright law?"

"What's the answer?" I asked.

"It's still being worked out in the courts," he answered. "Until recently, lawyers had little need for theology."

**

In the pool two waves meet and communicate. Other raindrops fall.

**

The cat lay prone in a support harness that kept its head immobile. The optic nerve of one of its eyes had been rerouted to electrodes extending from a nearby small computer.

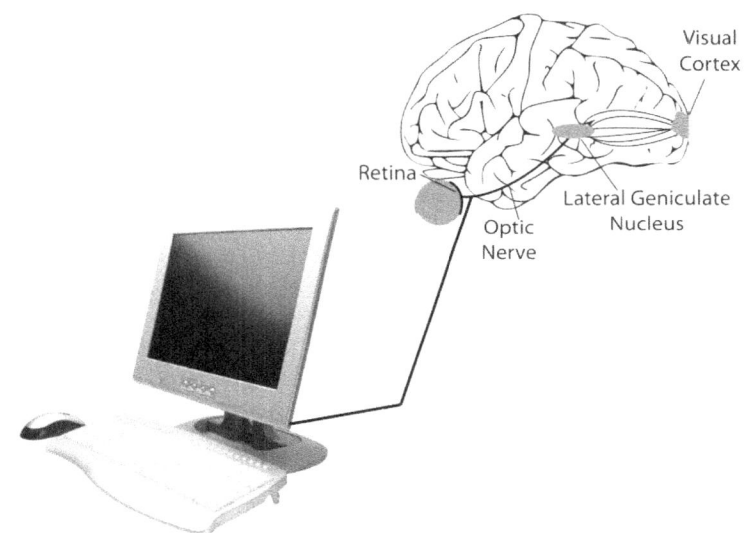

The students gathered around this cat had programmed the computer to mimic the signals coming from the cat's eye, and they watched the cat's brain as it responded to the imaginary world they created for it.

"Suppose that were me," asked a student. "If all my senses were hooked up to computers, how would I know that my experiences weren't real?"

"What do you mean real?" asked the professor.

"I mean real as in 'real world' as opposed to unreal as in 'video game'."

The professor thought for a moment and then answered, "I think you're asking the wrong question. It's not a matter of real versus unreal; it's a matter of hardware versus software. My nervous system tells me a story and I manufacture and live in a universe more or less consistent with those stories. My universe is entirely software — information sent to me along pathways I call nerve cells. I can't know where those pathways terminate. Perhaps they terminate in real eyes, ears, fingers, and toes. Perhaps they terminate in the running program of some very large computer or computer network. Perhaps they terminate in something beyond my comprehension.

"I live in the software. The hardware may be unknowable."

> Ever since Pascal and Leibnitz, people have dreamt of machines that could perform intellectual tasks. In the nineteenth century, Boole and DeMorgan devised "laws of thought" — essentially the Propositional Calculus — and thus took the first step towards AI [Artificial Intelligence] software; also Charles Babbage designed the first "calculating engine" — the precursor to the hardware of computers and hence of AI. One could define AI as coming into existence at the moment when mechanical devices took over any tasks previously performable only by human minds. It is hard to look back and imagine the feelings of those who first saw toothed wheels performing additions and multiplications of large numbers. Perhaps they experienced a sense of awe at seeing "thoughts" flow in their very physical hardware. In any case, we do know that nearly a century later, when the first electronic computers were constructed, their inventors did experience an awesome and mystical sense of being in the presence of another kind of "thinking being". To what extent real thought was taking place was a source of much puzzlement; and even now, several decades later, the question remains a great source of stimulation and vitriolics. [2]

**

It's raining heavily now and the pools are alive with complex patterns. As the pools grow bigger they send out connecting streams. Lightning flashes across the sky, its light reflected in the pools of rain. I turn away from the tent opening and arrange my gear for the night. The sounds of the storm follow me.

**

"Where's the cat?" the student asked.

"In there," the professor pointed to a small box. "I thought we'd work with a simulated cat today."

"But why the box?" asked the student. "Why not just program the cat into the computer — the world and the cat that watches it can be part of the same program."

"Good point," the professor reflects. "An entire world in software!"

> The sun beat down through a sky that had never seen clouds. The winds swept across an earth as smooth as glass. Night never came, and autumn never gave way to winter. It never rained. The simulated weather in Edward Lorenz's new electronic computer changed slowly but certainly, drifting through a permanent dry midday midseason, as if the world had turned into Camelot, or some particularly bland version of southern California.
>
> Outside his window Lorenz could watch real weather, the early-morning fog creeping along the Massachusetts Institute of Technology campus or the low clouds slipping over the rooftops from the Atlantic. Fog and clouds never arose in the model running on his computer. The machine, a Royal McBee, was a thicket of wiring and vacuum tubes that occupied an ungainly portion of Lorenz's office, made a surprising and irritating noise, and broke down every week or so. It had neither the speed nor the memory to manage a realistic simulation of the earth's atmosphere and oceans. Yet Lorenz created a toy weather in 1960 that succeeded in mesmerizing his colleagues. Every minute the machine marked the passing of a day by printing a row of numbers across a page. If you know how to read the printouts, you would see a prevailing westerly wind swing now to the north, now to the south, now back to

the north. Digitized cyclones spun slowly around an idealized globe. As word spread through the department, the other meteorologists would gather around with the graduate students making bets on what Lorenz's weather would do next. Somehow, nothing ever happened the same way twice. [3]

**

I hear the rain beat against the taut nylon above my head.

"I'm alive," I say to the storm.

I remember a poem.

> I lay on my bed
> Beneath a tin roof
> And listen to the rain think. [4]

"I'm alive," I say to the storm.

~~

[1] A.M. Turing, Computing Machinery and Intelligence. Mind, Vol. LIX, No. 236 (1950).

[2] Douglas R. Hofstadter, Godel, Escher, Bach: an Eternal Golden Braid (New York, Basic Books, 1979), 600–601.

[3] James Gleick, Chaos: Making a New Science. (New York, Viking, 1987), 11-12.

[4]Japanese haiku. I think Basho, but I've lost the reference.

10 SOFTWARE

Her eyes are open; her mind is alert. She almost died earlier today, and when she awoke from that episode she could no longer talk. Now she speaks with her eyes, and her fear is gone — replaced with what seems to be a bewildered serenity.

**

The three of us would meet every few months to discuss our book, and to design the computer simulations that were such an important part of it. We would lose ourselves for hours in the imaginary world we were creating, and which we hoped might serve students as a map to a small part of the real world — whatever, wherever that is.

One of us had once been the student of one of the world's great scientists, and he sometimes joined this man for dinner immediately after our meetings. I was invited to join the two of them several times, but never found the courage to accept. Not only was this man a great scientist, but he was an even greater character. I simply could not overcome my shyness with respect to such a real human being.

When he died I thought that a door slammed shut behind me, and that I would never meet him.

Several months later I found his autobiography in a bookstore. As I read his stories it was as if parts of his personality transferred themselves into my brain. The book repeatedly triggered in me unfolding cascades of memory and emotion. While it's possible that this man wrote his words from a different place, a different universe of feelings, it is my myth that he triggered in me some of the attitudes and feelings that had once been him. It was as if his book had programmed a portion of my brain — shaping it into rooms where he might comfortably live.

These sensations lasted only a few months and then, once again, my mind seemed wholly my own. Still, every once in a while, I look inside to see if he's there. He's welcome anytime.

**

Something is happening. She looks at me with a slight frown, as if asking a question.

"Come back any time," I say. "There's always room for you in here."

She smiles.

"I love you," I say.

She closes her eyes.

She stops breathing.

11 STONES, ORDER, …

"Ready to climb," my partner says.

We're standing in the boulder field at the base of the seven hundred foot granite cliff we've chosen for the morning's climb. My partner, a geologist I've known since graduate school, looks up at the wall with appreciation and delight.

"You're on belay," I respond ritually.

I look at the array of chocks, carabiners, and brightly colored nylon loops that are arranged on a sling across his shoulder, and then examine the purple climbing rope that extends from his harness to my gloved right hand. From my right hand the rope passes behind my body, across my buttocks, through the glove of my left hand, and into a neat pile of circular loops at my feet before terminating in a bowline knot in the front of my harness.

"Climbing," he says.

"Climb away," I answer.

**

"The second law of thermodynamics is often used to point the direction of all real events in time," my high school science teacher argued. "Suppose that I show you a film of a hammer and a pitcher of water. I run the film; you see the hammer come into your field of view and touch the pitcher; you see the pitcher fragment and the water spill; you see the hammer lying in the wet debris. I run the film again but this time you see the hammer retrieved from a wet pile of debris; you see water and fragments of glass assemble themselves into a pitcher of water at the hammer's tip; you see the hammer withdrawn.

"In which case did I run the film forward? In which case did I run the film in reverse?"

My teacher remained silent for a moment, but didn't really expect an answer to his question.

"Obviously, the film is running in the right direction when you see things wear out, break down, move from order to disorder. One way of viewing the second law of thermodynamics is to say that, when taken as a whole, the universe has a continual tendency to move towards greater randomness.

"In other words," he joked, "it is a law of nature that, from our perspective, things go from bad to worse.

With these words, I remembered Douglas Spaulding.

"It's been a tough summer," Tom said. "Lots of things have happened to Doug."

"Tell me about them," said the junkman.

"Well," said Tom, gasping for breath, not quite done crying yet, "He lost his best aggie for one, a real beaut. And on top of that somebody stole his catcher's mitt, it cost a dollar ninety-five. Then there was the bad trade he made of his fossil stones and shell collection with Charlie Woodman for a Tarzan clay statue you got by saving up macaroni box tops. Dropped the Tarzan statue on the sidewalk second day he had it."

"That's a shame," said the junkman and really saw all the pieces on the cement.

"Then he didn't get the book of magic tricks he wanted for his birthday, got a pair of pants and a shirt instead. That's enough to ruin the summer right there."

"Parents sometimes forget how it is," said Mr. Jonas.

"Sure," Tom continued in a low voice, "then Doug's genuine set of Tower-of-London manacles left out all night and rusted. And worst of all, I grew one inch taller, catching up with him almost."

"Is that all?" asked the junkman quietly.

"I could think of ten dozen other things, all as bad or worse. Some summers you get a run of luck like that. It's been silver fish getting into his comics collection or mildew in his new tennis shoes ever since Doug got out of school."

"I remember years like that," said the junkman.

He looked off at the sky and there were all the years.

"So there you are, Mr. Jonas. That's it. That's why he's dying …" [1]

It's funny how a bit of science can trigger such a personal response, but the second law of thermodynamics became a Secret of the Universe for me that day.

**

I follow my friend's movement up the chimney and out onto the face of the rock. Behind me, below the boulder field, I hear the sounds of the forest.

**

"It is a popular myth," my professor was saying, "that living systems disobey the second law of thermodynamics. According to the second law, spontaneous processes always involve transformations in which disorder, the entropy of the system, increases.

"However, if I were to show you a time-lapse film of a germinating seedling, you would see an elaborate and complex system build itself before your eyes. You would see disorder decreasing rather than increasing — the exact opposite of a breaking glass or a diffusing gas.

"Life, of course, isn't spontaneous. To sustain life, enormous amounts of energy are required." We all laughed as he took a large bite out of his Snicker's bar.

On the corner of his desk a lidded, glass container was filled with a violet-colored gas.

"This beaker contains molecules of a harmless gas that, for the moment, are separated from the air we're breathing. There is an ordering in this room such that the gas molecules are inside the beaker but not outside. If I gently remove the lid, and stand back …"

As we watched, the violet color in the beaker slowly faded and disappeared.

"Before our eyes," the professor continued, "a small aspect of our universe has spontaneously moved from an ordered to a disordered state.

"There is no law, of course, that states that we can't restore that order by using some chemical process to recover the molecules of gas from the air in this room and return them to the beaker. All it takes is energy." He took another bite from his candy.

"Life on this planet has sustained the evolution of increasingly ordered systems because it has access to an enormous energy supply — our Sun. That energy is used to drive the chemical processes that define life as we presently know it."

Perhaps Douglas will live after all, I thought.

> "At seven-thirty Mrs. Spaulding came out of the back door to empty some watermelon rinds into the garbage pail and saw Mr. Jonas standing there.
> "How is the boy?" said Mr. Jonas.
> Mrs. Spaulding stood there for a moment, a response trembling on her lips.
> "May I see him, please?" said Mr. Jonas.
> Still she could say nothing.

"I know the boy well," he said. "Seen him most every day of his life since he was out and around. I've something for him in the wagon."

"He's not —" She was going to say "conscious," but she said, "awake. He's not awake, Mr. Jonas. The doctor said he's not to be disturbed. Oh, we don't know what's wrong!"

"Even if he's not 'awake'" said Mr. Jonas. "I'd like to talk to him. Sometimes the things you hear in your sleep are more important, you listen better, it gets through." [2]

"Of course," my professor finished. "The sun will burn out eventually."

"I'm sorry, Mr. Jonas, I just can't take the chance." Mrs. Spaulding caught hold of the screen-door handle and held fast to it. "Thanks. Thank you, anyway, for coming by."

"Yes, ma'am," said Mr. Jonas. [3]

**

My friend has reached a narrow ledge seventy-five feet up the wall.

"Off belay," he shouts down.

"Belay off," I respond.

I take a long look at the extraordinary shapes in this granite cliff. The cracks and fractures in the rock form a sculpture of enormous beauty and challenge.

"This is no disordered bit of chaos," I think to myself. "Every rock I've ever climbed has been my teacher.

"Ready to climb," I shout.

"You're on belay," my partner calls down.

"Climbing."

"Climb away," he answers.

**

"The second law of thermodynamics is helpful in understanding the behavior of steam engines and the direction of chemical reactions," my colleague told me. "It definitely does not offer insight about the universe as a whole or the tragedy of our place in it."

I was stunned. A Secret of the Universe, defamed?

My colleague and I were sitting before his Macintosh computer and putting the final touches on a program we were writing to drill college students on the nature of chemical equilibrium.

"Excuse me?"

"Think about it," he responded. "The idea that the universe as a whole is continually running downhill, from order to disorder, is totally contrary to the observations of any honest observer. The universe as a whole — both living and unliving — is continually moving towards a state of greater, not lesser, order.

"Stars evolve, form intricately interacting clusters, galaxies, and when they die they spew a rich mixture of heavier elements into their neighborhood that permit the evolution of even more complex stellar systems.

"Planets evolve — starting out as balls of undifferentiated debris that ultimately form complex masses with surfaces that are often marked by highly ordered mountains, streams, hills, and valleys; and whose interiors are extensively differentiated by density and by mineral type.

"When you look at the real world, at any scale and in any way, whether by simple visual observation or with the aid of the most sophisticated tools of crystallography, geology, and astronomy, you will find not disorder, but order.

"A general drive toward disorder simply does not exist."
[4]

"But life …," I interjected.

"… participates in the evolution towards greater order just like everything else, only more quickly," he answered.

"I don't understand," I rushed in. "Are you saying that the second law of thermodynamics is wrong."

"No," he answered. "I'm saying that it's misunderstood. It simply doesn't apply to many of the settings where metaphor has placed it."

"Look," I fought back. "If I open a closed container of some gas, it disperses; it doesn't spontaneously order itself into a cloud sculpture."

"Keep going," he laughed.

"That's it," I answered. "It disperses and that's the end of it."

"And these molecules of gas just keep dispersing out past the orbit of the moon heading towards Alpha Centauri?" he asked.

I began to feel a disquieting confusion. "Well, no. There's gravity. Most don't escape the gravitational field of the Earth."

"That's the point," he concluded. "The second law of thermodynamics doesn't take into account all of the energy flows in the universe. If a spoonful of coffee grounds is stirred into a thermos of water, the resulting random suspension will quickly change to a more ordered state — the coffee grounds settle to the bottom of the cup.

"Gravity helps coffee grounds to settle, stars and galaxies to form, planets to evolve, atmospheres to form and nourish life.

"The universe is a dynamic system, containing energy flows of many types, not just those of classical thermodynamics. Each of these energy flows can generate order, and many do."

Mr. Jonas swayed in indecision, looked at the bottles he carried, made his decision, and moved forward stealthily to sit on the grass and look at this boy crushed down by the great weight of summer.

"Doug," he said, "you just lie quiet. You don't have to say anything or open your eyes. You don't even have to pretend to listen. But inside there, I know you hear me, and it's old Jonas, your friend. Your friend," he repeated and nodded.

He reached up and picked an apple off the tree, turned it round, took a bite, chewed, and continued.

...

"Well, now, where are we?" he asked.

"A hot night, not a breath stirring, in August," he answered himself. "Killing hot. And a long summer it's been and too much happening, eh? Too much. And it's getting on toward one o'clock and no sign of a wind or rain. And in a moment now I'm going to get up and go. But when I go, and remember this clearly, I will leave these two bottles here upon your bed. And when I've gone I want you to wait a little while and then slowly open your eyes and sit up and reach over and drink the contents of these bottles. Not with your mouth, no. Drink with your nose. Tilt the bottles, uncork them, and let what is in them go right down into your head. Read the labels first, of course."

...

A moment later there was the sound of reins slapping the back of the horse in the moonlight, and the rumble of the wagon down the street and away.

After a moment Douglas's eyes twitched and, very slowly, opened. [5]

**

"Do you think that there's a purpose to all of this?" I ask my friend. We've finished our climb and stand at the cliff's edge looking out at infinity.

"You think too much," my friend laughs.

"But this constant striving towards order. Doesn't it tell you that there's a purpose to it all?"

My friend pauses, turns slowly, and looks deeply into my

eyes.

"You still don't get it, do you," he says.

The moment's silence lasts forever.

"We still have a long way to go," he says, slapping me on the back.

We assemble our gear and walk away from the edge of the cliff and into the forest behind.

~~

[1] Ray Bradbury, Dandelion Wine (Garden City, Doubleday & Company, Inc., 1957), 253-255.

[2] Ray Bradbury, Dandelion Wine (Garden City, Doubleday & Company, Inc., 1957), 255-256.

[3] Ray Bradbury, Dandelion Wine (Garden City, Doubleday & Company, Inc., 1957), 256.

[4] This entire conversation has been paraphrased from an untitled, unpublished manuscript of Daniel E. Atkinson (University of California, Los Angeles), Chapter 1, Order and Entropy.

[5] Ray Bradbury, Dandelion Wine (Garden City, Doubleday & Company, Inc., 1957), 258–259.

12 …RESPONSIBILITY

"Who's responsible?" the voice asks.

I arrived in this meadow early in the day and spent the afternoon breathing its silence. A carpet of new snow has erased the incoming tracks of my cross country skis, and I sit alone in the center of an uninhabited universe.

"You mean what's responsible, don't you?"

"Do I?" the voice laughs.

**

"The end of World War II saw the influx of large numbers of physicists to biology," the instructor mused. "Many, I think, were hoping to find some new 'force', some new principle unnoticed by the observers of non-living systems. To date, of course, they have failed. Most would now agree that living systems follow exactly the same rules as non-living systems, and that life exploits no 'secret force' that is unavailable to its inanimate cousins."

The speaker was a summer instructor at a venerable marine biology laboratory nestled in a harbor on Cape Cod, Massachusetts. Outside our windows were anchored the specimen boats of the laboratory, and the larger deep-ocean vessels of a neighboring oceanographic institute. The air was rich with salt and the slight tang of decay that always accompanies low tide.

"These physicists failed in their quest for a holy grail. Instead, they brought the grail with them — mathematics, physics, chemistry."

Those of us listening to the instructor were advanced graduate students or newly minted postdoctoral fellows. This summer was meant to give us "perspective" on our discipline.

"Consider the problem of embryonic development. For many species, a single fertilized egg divides over and over again until it forms a hollow mass of cells. These cells then migrate in an orderly fashion to new locations within the mass to sculpt the rough outlines of a new, living organism — skin on the outside, gut on the inside."

Skin   Gut

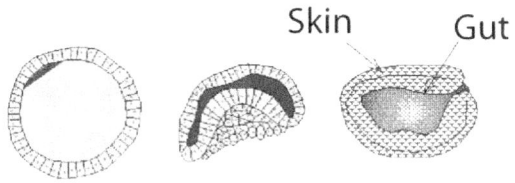

"It is tempting when viewing such motions to imagine forces at work that are outside the realm of physical science. We now believe, however, that such motions are really no more complex than the motions that separate water from oil. In experimental systems, we find that cells at the interior of differentiating cell masses have surfaces with greater strengths of adhesion than those on the outside. While, there are probably many different physical processes that direct the motion of living cells, I believe that we will find that all such processes are grounded in physics — and relatively simple physics at that." [1]

**

The temperature and humidity in this meadow have changed and a wind has risen. The texture of the snow is changing and patterns like sand dunes are forming in the field before me. As the sun lowers and shadows lengthen, the snow seems almost to be alive.

**

"Your embryos are like my galaxies," my companion said. He was an astronomer on loan to the oceanographic institute for some unfathomable reason. We sat on the dock of the institute and watched the crew of a tender prepare its small, two-person submarine for the next day's departure.

"What do you mean?" I asked.

"This constant push towards increasing order — in galaxies, in stars, in living creatures — depends upon a quite remarkable set of coincidences. If the gravitational constant of our universe or if the chemistry of carbon atoms, for example, were only slightly different than they are, the whole intricate machine would fall apart.

"I don't know of any reason why G must be 6.67×10^{-11} N m^2kg^{-2} or why other physical constants must have values that yield carbon atoms that can form long chains. What if they didn't? There are a hundred attributes of the universe that must be exactly as they are in order for things to work with such clockwork precision. Change just a few of them and 'Good bye, Universe.'"

"Or, perhaps," I said, "hello to a different but equally interesting universe."

"I don't think so," he answered, "Change a few universal

constants and things simply don't work together. Period. It's not a subjective thing. The universe consists of a set of rules and physical constants that are wildly improbable; yet, without them, we wouldn't be here."

"Are you proposing this as a proof for the existence of God?" I asked.

"Of course not," he joked. "I'm offering it as proof of the non-existence of us."

**

The sun is at the horizon and flames of orange light ignite the meadow in an act of creation. Should I be here to see this? Is it permitted?

**

"It's a simple exercise, really," he explained. "You point a telescope at the sky and measure the location of every star and its direction of travel. It turns out that the stars are all moving away from each other. It's as if you marked the surface of a balloon with ink spots and then began to pump more air into it. Every dot on the surface of the balloon moves away from every other dot. Visualize that in three dimensions instead of two and you have our universe."

"And if you run the movie backwards?" I asked.

"Then every star in the universe converges toward a single point in the center of the 'balloon'. Somewhere between thirteen and sixteen billion years ago everything in our universe was in the same place!"

"Must have been crowded," I suggested.

"You can't imagine!" he laughed. "An entire universe — super dense, super-hot — explodes away from a single location no larger than a golf ball. People are calling it 'The

Big Bang.'"

**

The sun is below the horizon and broad strokes of purple and red light surround me, permeate me, and place me at the center of creation.

"Are you ready?" the voice asks.

**

"And so he proposes that there were an infinite number of Big Bangs, all at the same moment?" I asked incredulously.

"Or at least a very large number," she answered. "It solves the problem of all those coincidences."

"Excuse me?"

"Don't you get it? A trillion-trillion different universes all get started at the moment of the Big Bang, and each of them has a different compilation of physical laws and universal constants. Most of them fizzle on the spot because the mix of laws and constants don't gel. Such universes, at best, lead a weak and uninteresting existence. One universe, or a few, however, gets it exactly right and the subsequent drive towards order leads to the evolution of us."

"And now we sit around in amazement at how perfectly suited the universe is to the evolution of conscious life. …"

"… While all those other universes," she interrupted, "don't have anybody in them to complain that the systems don't work."

"So the early Christian Church was right after all," I mused.

"What?" she asked.

"The Church placed man at the center of God's universe and got very upset when Copernicus (and, more especially, Galileo) told it that man was not at the center. General relativity comes along and says that it's really all relative and you can choose any center you wish, and now you tell me that we are at the center. By looking out at our universe we verify its existence as a coherent, working system."

"Who decides what's coherent and working?" she retorted.

"We do!" I laughed. [2]

**

The fires are gone, and stars are beginning to appear. Out on the snow field the wind whips up crystals of ice and sends them playing across the dunes. Soon moonlight will shine on this meadow and flashing spirits of ice will pray to the wind.

"How do you feel?" the voice asks.

"I don't know," I answer. "I'm thinking about an alchemist who saw creation in a spreading cloud of consecrated wine."

"That's a good start," the voice says gently.

~~

[1] An excellent discussion of the physics of embryonic cell movement can be found in Steinberg, M.S., Does differential adhesion govern self-assembly processes in histogenesis? Equilibrium configurations and the emergence of a hierarchy among populations of embryonic cells. Journal of Experimental Zoology vol. 173, pp. 395–433 (1970).

[2] Physicists call it the anthropic principle. You can read about it in: Barrow, John D. and Frank J. Tipler, The Anthropic Cosmological Principle (New York, Oxford

University Press, 1986); or in Breuer, Reinhard A., The Anthropic Principle : Man as the Focal Point of Nature (Boston, Birkhauser, 1991).

13 MIRACLES

Strong winds whip clouds of white powder snow across our trail and it is difficult to see.

"How much further?" I ask.

"There's the tree line," she points. "The cabin is just inside on the left."

We've been up on the ice for three days. It will be nice to be warm again.

**

"Who's responsible?" I asked.

"Excuse me?" the priest looked at me with a smile.

"You're a biologist — an expert in evolutionary theory — and you're a priest. Who has the last word?"

Lunch at the faculty club had preceded this tour of the campus, and my host had put me at ease masterfully. I was asking questions to which I really wanted answers.

"God has the last word," he laughed. "Who else?"

It was late autumn and a stiff breeze sent swirls of colored leaves about our ankles as we walked past well-kept lawns and dark stone buildings. The residents of this celebrated institution entranced me — especially the dark clad priests who worked side by side with their often quite secular colleagues.

"For me, the study of natural selection and evolution is a means rather than an end," he volunteered. "In the path from self-replicating molecules to thinking beings more happens than a reshuffling of DNA. Order emerges, and consciousness evolves to observe and value that order. The biologist in me studies the evolution of life; the priest studies the evolution of spirit."

My mind rushed to memories of a man named George — who made a pact with the devil.

> There are different ways to look at things.
>
> The way psychiatrists are most accustomed to understand human beings is in terms of health and disease. This viewpoint is known as the medical model. It is a very useful and effective way of looking at people.
>
> According to this viewpoint, George was suffering from a very specific disease — namely, an obsessive-compulsive neurosis. We know a good deal about this disease. In many ways George's case was typical.
>
> ...
>
> The problem is that, viewed in this light, the relationship between George and the devil seems prosaic and not very significant. How would it seem if we viewed it instead in terms of a traditional Christian religious model?
>
> According to this model, humanity (and perhaps the entire universe) is locked in a titanic struggle between the forces of good and evil, between God and the devil. The battleground of this struggle is the individual human soul. The entire meaning of human life revolves around the battle. The only question of ultimate significance is whether the individual soul will be won to God or won to the devil. By establishing through his pact a relationship with the devil, George had placed his soul in the greatest jeopardy known to man. It was clearly the critical point in his life. And possibly even the fate of all humanity turned upon his decision. Choirs of angels and armies of demons were watching him, hanging on his every thought, praying continually for one outcome or the other. [1]

"You have the idea, " the priest mused. "Human beings are important! We have a job to do!"

**

"I can't see the trail," I call.

The wind has churned the snow into a maelstrom of blinding, chilling, fog. My companion, a ranger with the forest service, is barely visible just a few feet ahead. She reaches back for my hand.

"We can't stop here." she shouts. "I know where we are. Just a little further."

**

"The Bible has a history," my professor was saying, "but there are times when that history is unclear and our understanding must be tempered with speculation. Consider the miracle of the loaves and the fishes."

> In those days, when again a great crowd had gathered, and they had nothing to eat, he called his disciples to him, and said to them, "I have compassion on the crowd, because they have been with me now three days, and have nothing to eat; and if I send them away hungry to their homes, they will faint on the way; and some of them have come a long way." And his disciples answered him, "How can one feed these men with bread here in the desert?" And he asked them, "How many loaves have you?" They said, "Seven." And he commanded the crowd to sit down on the ground; and he took the seven loaves, and having given thanks he broke them and gave them to his disciples to set before the people; and they set them before the crowd. And they had a few small fish; and having blessed them, he commanded that these also should be set before them. And they ate, and were satisfied; and they took up the broken pieces left over, seven baskets full. And there

were about four thousand people. [2]

"What do you think?" he asked the class. "Do you think that Jesus had some kind of a matter transmuter that turned stone into food? And would his access to advanced technology make him worthy of your devotion as a spiritual leader?

Silence.

"The Bible gives us the result, not the method. Personally, I think that real miracles change hearts, not molecular structures. I like to think that Jesus knew that his command to share seven loaves and a few small fish would help others in the crowd to stop hoarding their own hidden supplies of food."

**

"The door's locked," I shout to my friend. "We can't get in."

The snow has given way to a freezing rain. My bones are cold, my spirit exhausted.

"The key's in the depression in the beam over the door," she shouts. "Everyone knows that."

**

The room was deserted. A popular exhibit elsewhere in the museum had left me alone with this carving — a woodcut from the early middle ages. The card said only "Heaven and Hell."

The lower panel was obviously Hell. A group of people sat before a large table laden with food. Their left hands were tied behind their backs and their right wrists were secured to their right shoulders. Large spoons, perhaps three feet long, extended from their right hands to the food, but there seemed to be no way to get the food from spoon to mouth. Everyone at the table was hungry.

The upper panel was obviously Heaven. A group of people sat before a large table laden with food. Their left hands were tied behind their backs and their right wrists were secured to their right shoulders. Large spoons, perhaps three feet long, extended from their right hands to the food. They were feeding each other.

**

Outside the wind howls and the rain beats on the windows of the cabin. Someone has stacked dry wood just inside the door. Some of it now burns in a well-kept, pot-bellied stove. A note near the wood says, "Weather permitting, gather more before you leave." In my mind I contrast the hospitality of this cabin with the storm outside.

She looks up and smiles.

I smile back.

We both listen to the storm.

~~

[1] M. Scott Peck, People of the Lie: The Hope for Healing Human Evil (New York, Simon and Schuster, 1983), 36–38.

[2] The Gospel According to Mark 8: 1–9 (The Holy Bible, Revised Standard Edition, Thomas Nelson & Sons, 1946, 1952).

14 FUGUE

"What do you hear?" he asks.
"Thunder," I answer.
"Laughter," his wife answers.
"A waterfall," says the little girl.

**

"I don't believe it!" the social worker said. "We've got thirty thousand homeless people in this town and the city's solution is to nail two by fours to the park benches so that they're uncomfortable to lie on."

"What do you want us to do?" responded the councilman's representative. "Everyone else is being driven out of the parks."

The senior administrator of the hospital that had called this meeting, a Catholic nun, listened attentively, but her eyes were focused on something on the wall behind me.

"I want you to …"

"Excuse me," the nun interrupted.

Everyone fell silent.

"We will take a short break. I would like you all to return to the table with a list of both your resources and your needs. Thank you."

She then returned to contemplation of the wall behind me.

As the meeting broke up into smaller groups, I glanced at this wall and saw that it was bare except for a crucifix and, clearly separated, a painting of an old man riding an ox. The ox stood looking contentedly to its left; the old man searched the heavens as if seeking something lost. When I reached down to retrieve my papers I noticed the nun smiling at me.

"An interesting picture, don't you think," she said. "What do you suppose the old man has lost?"

I laughed, because I knew this painting.

"The ox, I think."

She looked me in the eye, smiled, and then returned to contemplating the picture.

Several days later a small package arrived in the mail. It contained a book of Zen koans written by a Jesuit priest teaching at a Catholic university in Japan. Inside the front cover was a carefully penned inscription:

> You may be right.
>
> Sister M_

**

The little girl runs up the trail beside the waterfall, laughing. My friends and I trail behind at a slower pace.

**

The kung-an of Po-chang Huai-hai solved! [1]

"I'm tired," I said.

"It's three o'clock in the morning," she replied.

The experiment required samples to be taken every three hours for several days. I had put a cot in the lab and had been living on Coke, pretzels, and an occasional hamburger. The second night, in front of the cafeteria vending machines, I discovered that I was not alone in the building. We were in her lab where she was applying tiny samples of dissolved membrane to an electrophoresis gel. On the wall behind the work bench was a picture of an old man riding an ox. The ox stood looking contentedly to its left; the old man searched the heavens for something lost.

"What's the old man looking for?" I asked.

"His ox," she answered.

I laughed.

"Would you like to know a secret?" she asked.

"Sure."

"Stand over by the centrifuge and look at the picture from there."

I walked over to the centrifuge and discovered that, from this perspective, it seemed as if the man had found his ox. He was looking down in calm bewilderment. As I moved forward to see what trick of light caused this phenomenon the ox and then the man disappeared.

"Amazing isn't it," she said.

I went back to my chair and sat looking at the man riding his ox.

"Now that you've seen it," she said, "you must promise to tell everyone you know."

**

We're above the waterfall and walking along the shore of a small mountain lake. The current is imperceptible, the air still. Who would know what energies are nearby?

**

"Aldous Huxley," my professor said, "divided religions into two types — historical and perennial. [2] Historical religions are those that declare God to be a conscious entity that intervenes directly in human affairs by curing a leper or parting the Red Sea. According to Huxley, such religions have a dogma that instructs humanity in its role in fulfilling God's purpose. He offered Judaism, Christianity, and Islam as examples.

"Perennial religions are much more difficult to pin down because words can't be used to describe them. No matter what you say, it is wrong; no matter what you see, it is illusion. There is no dogma, there is no God; there is no purpose. There is only mystery. He offered Buddhism and Taoism as examples.

"Actually, all religions have both historical and perennial components. There is a dogma that guides adherents to right actions and right thoughts, and there is a mystical tradition that guides a small number of adherents into mystery. To approach mystery you must meditate — upon paradox or in silence.

THE CASE

The priest Hsiang-yen said, "It is as though you were up in a tree, hanging from a branch with your teeth. Your hands and feet can't touch any branch. Someone appears beneath the tree and asks, "What is the meaning of Bodhidharma's coming from the West?" If you do not answer, you evade your responsibility. If you do answer, you lose your life. What do you do?"

WU-MEN'S COMMENT

Even if your eloquence flows like a river, it is all in vain. Even if you can expound cogently upon the whole body of Buddhist literature, that too is useless. If you can respond to this dilemma properly, you give life to those who have been dead and kill those who have been alive. If you can't respond, you must wait and ask Maitreya about it.

WU-MEN'S VERSE

Hsiang-yen is just babbling nonsense;
His poisonous intentions are limitless.
He stops up the monks' mouths,
Making his whole body a demon eye.[3]

**

My friends and I prepare lunch while watching the little

girl play at the edge of the lake. She laughs. The water splashes. Do they know each other?

**

He taught neuroanatomy at the medical school and he was a world class harpsichordist. The sitting room held almost thirty people ... and his harpsichord.

"I'm going to play 'The Art of the Fugue' by Bach," he said. "Fugues are similar to canons in that different voices of a single theme are played against themselves in different keys and at different speeds. Sometimes it is even possible to play the same theme forward and backward simultaneously — the mirrored voices singing to each other in marvelous harmony.

"It has always struck me as remarkable that music can sometimes spring from the apposition of apparently irreconcilable opposites."

He sat down before his instrument and, almost as an afterthought, turned to address his audience one more time.

"Bach was a very religious man. Both the historical and the perennial God exist in this music. They co-exist happily. The contradiction is unimportant, only the music matters."

And then he began to play, and he was right.

At one time during the performance I noticed his hands. They moved totally independently. They seemed to play unrelated bits of music — different notes, different rhythms. But in my ears I heard a single piece.

He continued his performance the next morning in his neuroanatomy lecture for first-year medical students. Before him was a blackboard. In its tray was every possible color of chalk. He picked up different colors in each hand

and began to draw. Sometimes his hands worked in concert — to complete symmetrical arcs or other shapes — but often they worked independently. One hand would draw the posterior columns of the spinal cord while the other hand reached down, selected a color, and returned to draw an anterior motor neuron.

In three minutes his drawing was complete. He turned and bowed. The students cheered.

"How can you do that," one student asked.

"I never stop to think," he answered.

> And so we began again from the very beginning, as if everything I had learned hitherto had become useless. But the waiting at the point of highest tension was no more successful than before, as if it were impossible for me to get out of the rut.
>
> One day I asked the Master: "How can the shot be loosed if 'I' do not do it?"
>
> "'It' shoots," he replied.
>
> "I have heard you say that several times before, so let me put it another way: How can I wait self-obliviously for the shot if 'I' am no longer there?"
>
> "'It' waits at the highest tension."
>
> "And who or what is this 'It'?"
>
> "Once you have understood that, you will have no further need of me. And if I tried to give you a clue at the cost of your own experience, I would be the worst of teachers and would deserve to be sacked! So let's stop talking about it and go on practicing." [4]

∗∗

The little girl is asleep and my friends and I sit silently, watching her. There is nothing to say.

~~

[1] Willard Johnson, Riding the Ox Home: A History of Meditation from Shamanism to Science. (Rider & Company, London, 1982).

[2] Aldous Huxley, The Perennial Philosophy. (London, Chatto & Windus, 1957).

[3] Robert Aitkin (trans), The Gateless Barrier: The Wu-Men Kuan (Mumonkan). (San Francisco, North Point Press, 1990), 38.

[4] Eugen Herrigel, Zen in the Art of Archery. (New York, Vintage Books, 1989), 51–52.

15 WAKING

It's dark — I hear water rushing in a nearby stream and smell the pine of the surrounding forest. I roll to one side and notice that the ground beneath me is unusually soft — a bed actually. I seem to be in two places at once. I'm surrounded by the sounds and smells of wilderness, but feel the touch of my bed in Los Angeles. Am I dreaming? Which part is the dream?

**

"People of God must tend seriously to their inner lives," my professor was saying, "but, for most, the religious life also requires action. Consider this passage from the Old Testament."

> One day Jonathan the son of Saul said to the young man who bore his armor, "Come, let us go over to the Philistine garrison on yonder side. But he did not tell his father.
> ...
> And there was a panic in the [Philistine] camp, in the field, and among all the people; the garrison and even the raiders trembled; the earth quaked, and it became a great panic.

> And the watchmen of Saul in Gibeah of Benjamin looked; and behold, the multitude was surging hither and thither. Then Saul said to the people who were with him, "Number and see who has gone from us." And when they had numbered, behold, Jonathan and his armor bearer were not there. And Saul said to Ahijah, "Bring hither the ark of God." For the ark of God went at that time with the people of Israel. And while Saul was talking to the priest, the tumult in the camp of the Philistines increased more and more; and Saul said to the priest, "Withdraw your hand." Then Saul and all the people who were with him rallied and went into the battle; and behold, every man's sword was against his fellow, and there was very great confusion. [1]

"In this extraordinary passage," my professor continued, "Saul needed to act quickly, but also he needed to act according to God's will. At this time in their history, the Israelites carried with them the Ark of the Covenant (the ark of God). Within the Ark were objects used by the priests to divine the will of God. When Saul first suspected that his son was engaged in battle with the Philistines, he called for the Ark and asked the priest to ascertain God's will. As the tumult increased and the Philistine's panic became clear, however, he told the priest to withdraw his hand from the Ark, and Saul entered into battle before the usual signs and portends could be read!"

What would it be like, I asked myself, to live in a world in which my actions were important to God. And what would be the consequences of wrong action!

"Well?" my professor looked at me, sensing my dilemma. "How would you judge Saul's actions? Did Saul put his own will before God's, or did he seek God's will from another source — his enemy's panic?"

He shrugged.

"The Bible itself debates this question! To the writers of the earliest texts, the 'J' account of King David's court,

Saul's actions were correct. These writers tell us that God lives in history, and that a person of integrity can discover God's will in the events of history.

"To writers of the Diaspora, however, Saul's actions were wrong. Israel was no longer a sovereign nation, and its people were scattered throughout the known world. To keep these people together required a strong center. These writers tell us that Saul put his own wishes above the rule of the priest … and therefore above God."

I felt a knot tightening in my stomach. I didn't want this kind of responsibility. I looked up to see my professor watching me, concerned.

"The religious life is not an easy one," he said quietly. "It's not a game; the burdens are enormous; the dangers are very real."

**

Where am I? The rush of the nearby stream is compelling, but I can feel also the still form of a woman lying beside me in our bed. I hear her murmur softly from her sleep in a language I barely understand.

I remember a journey — long ago … or is it happening now for the first time, in a dream?

**

"It's time for you to go home," they say.

"This is my home," I protest.

We're camped in a high meadow at the foot of a glacier that dominates our western horizon. A stream of pale blue, almost phosphorescent water — unfiltered melt from ancient ice — rushes past me and gathers strength for its journey into the canyons below.

"From this place you can understand," the woman says quietly, "but you can't grow."

"These mountains," her husband interjects. "They can only be as big as you are."

"Go home."

"Change your life."

"Grow."

They laugh.

"And these mountains will grow with you!"

**

I awake to a terrible feeling of loss.

The room is dark; the sheets and comforter are gathered snugly around me and keep me warm.

"Are you all right?" the woman asks.

"A dream," I answer.

"Tell me about it," she moves closer.

"I can't remember," I say to her already sleeping form.

I lay in the bed for another hour until the first gray light of morning appears in the window.

I dress quickly and step out onto the balcony. A staircase descends to the narrow walkway that leads to the street. The sun rises above the horizon.

I walk down the stairs.

~~

[1] 1 Samuel 14: 1–20 (The Holy Bible, Revised Standard Edition, Thomas Nelson & Sons, 1946, 1952).

16 PAIN

The path skirts a grove of trees and descends to the lake, but it is this grove that I've been seeking. Years ago, among these trees, my friend would sit motionless for hours at a time.

I remember when, during a Christmas break, he told me that he had stopped meditating.

> "I'm giving it up," he said to me.
> "It?" I asked.
> "Meditation. I've stopped meditating."
>
> …
> "These last few months I've begun to experience things I can't describe. I've been standing at the edge of a place that is so still, so empty, so compelling, that I know if I go further I won't come back."

"I had forgotten you," I say softly. "Why suddenly do I remember?"

For a moment I almost remember a dream.

"What did you decide," I ask, "and where are you now?"

**

"Religion and psychology," my professor said, "are both

about changing the human soul — healing it; bringing it closer to what it wants to be."

He opened a book in front of him.

"Consider this," he said.

> As I worked with my fantasies, I became aware that the unconscious undergoes or produces change. Only after I had familiarized myself with alchemy did I realize that the unconscious is a process, and that the psyche is transformed or developed by the relationship of the ego to the contents of the unconscious. In individual cases that transformation can be read from dreams and fantasies. In collective life it has left its deposit principally in the various religious systems and their changing symbols. Through the study of these collective transformation processes and through understanding of alchemical symbolism I arrived at the central concept of my psychology: the process of individuation. [1]

"For many priests and ministers, of course, this is blasphemy. For many psychologists it is superstition. For me, however, it is the central experience of my life."

"What?" a student asked. "What is the central experience of your life?"

"Pain," he smiled.

**

It is mid-morning as I enter the old biology laboratories and pause to look into the museum that spans much of the first floor of the building. The bones of a dinosaur watch over me as I scan the rows of glass compartments with their fossils and their stones.

"Is there a process of evolution," I wonder, "for souls as well as planets. And is it as brutal?"

For a moment I feel clouds of thought and emotion chase each other behind my eyes. Do I hear a scream?

"Run, rabbit, run!" I whisper.

**

Her living room was festooned with a miscellany of objects collected over a lifetime. There was a photograph of her children on the mantle — dressed for the Arctic Sea and smiling from the deck of their fishing boat. They looked very young and very healthy.

She looked up at us from her sofa. "... Hi! ... Good ... ... to ... see ... ... you."

As we stood there we watched her body spasm and twitch. Her face grimaced and her head jerked to one side. Between these movements she looked calmly back at us — unembarrassed, almost serene.

My friend, a nurse, moved to her side and took her hand. "How are you?" she asked.

"... Good!" she said. "... Next ... week ... ... my ... children."

"Your children are coming to visit you?" she asked.

"... No! ... ... I ... visit ... ... them."

"To Alaska? Who's taking you?" my friend asked.

"... Myself! ..." she said, and laughed. "... I ... can ... do it!!"

> Life is difficult.
>
> ...
>
> What makes life difficult is that the process of confronting and solving problems is a painful one. Problems, depending upon their nature, evoke in us frustration or grief or sadness or loneliness or guilt or regret or anger or fear or anxiety or anguish or despair. These are uncomfortable feelings, often very uncomfortable, often as painful as any kind of physical pain, sometimes equaling the very worst kind of physical pain. Indeed, it is because of the pain that events or conditions engender in us all that we call them problems.

And since life poses an endless series of problems, life is always difficult and is full of pain as well as joy.

Yet it is in this whole process of meeting and solving problems that life has its meaning. Problems are the cutting edge that distinguishes between success and failure. Problems call forth our courage and our wisdom; indeed, they create our courage and our wisdom. [2]

*The first of the "Four Noble Truths" which Buddha taught was "Life is suffering."

"… You … want … … my … blood." she declared, holding out her arm.

"I want your blood," I laughed, as my friend opened her kit and prepared a syringe.

Years ago she, and many extraordinary others, had volunteered to help me with my studies of neurological disease. While alive they donated samples of blood and skin. When they died they offered their brains.

It took both of my hands and considerable strength to hold her arm still while my friend found a vein and withdrew the samples for my laboratory.

I looked up and saw her watching me.

"… You … … don't … like … … this!" she exclaimed.

"I don't like hurting you," I answered.

"… You … don't hurt … … me," she said looking at both of us. "You … … share … my … problem!"

A young woman brought in her breakfast as we finished our work. A man, perhaps the young woman's husband, stood watching from the door. They seemed haunted, ill at ease.

As we left the house I turned to my friend and asked, "Who were the young couple?"

"Her church sent them." she answered.

"Amazing!" I responded.

"Yes, but I don't think you get it," she laughed.

"Apparently that couple has been having some real problems. The church sent them here to get help."

> Of us all, Father was the only one who really had any kind of a faith. And I do not doubt that he had very much of it, and that behind the walls of his isolation, his intelligence and his will, unimpaired, and not hampered in any essential way by the partial obstruction of some of his senses, were turned to God, and communed with God. Who was with him and in him, and Who gave him, as I believe, light to understand and to make use of his suffering for his own good, and to perfect his soul. It was a great soul, large, full of natural charity. He was a man of exceptional intellectual honesty and sincerity and purity of understanding. And this affliction, this terrible and frightening illness which was relentlessly pressing him down even into the jaws of the tomb, was not destroying him after all.
>
> Souls are like athletes that need opponents worthy of them, if they are to be tried and extended and pushed to the full use of their powers, and rewarded according to their capacity. And my father was in a fight with his tumor, and none of us understood the battle. We thought he was done for, but it was making him great. [3]

**

My friend's laboratory is on the fourth floor, and I walk to the elevator before realizing that I returned my elevator key over twenty years ago.

Sorrow rises to my throat. I remember past dreams.

I turn toward the stairs.

**

"There are two kinds of pain," my professor said, "physical pain and psychic pain. Physical pain is a signal that something is wrong and, if possible, you should change your situation — take your hand out of the fire, pull the thorn out of your arm. Psychic pain is a signal that something is wrong and, if possible, you should change your situation — change your job, change your attitude.

"Curiously, while we seem to be very good at avoiding physical pain — it's very rare to find people who deliberately keep their hands in the fire — we appear less willing to avoid the sources of psychic pain. Indeed, we often appear to embrace them.

"Even among people with terminal illness it is often psychic pain that is the most devastating."

He walked to a window and stared out across the quadrangle.

"We don't like change," he said. "We don't understand that we must let go before we can move forward."

> "Your eviction notice came in the form of a great depression, a loss of the desire to live, just as it happened to us. When you told us that you didn't want to live, we couldn't help laughing."
> "What's going to happen to me now?" I asked.
> "Using the vernacular, you got to get another pad," don Juan replied. [4]

**

I leave the laboratories and turn left along a narrow, tree-lined, path.

"Where should I go now?" I ask myself. "What should I do?"

As the path opens up onto the street that leads to the Graduate College a brief moment of sanity shows me what I might become if only I could let go of the past. My mind fills with the memories of those I have known who disciplined their actions and changed their lives.

"That's ridiculous," I tell myself. "No one should be expected to be that strong."

"When a man starts to learn, he is never clear about his objectives. His purpose is faulty; his intent is vague. He hopes for rewards that will never materialize for he knows nothing about the hardships of learning.

"He slowly begins to learn — bit by bit at first, then in big chunks. And his pictures soon clash. What he learns is never what he pictured, or imagined, and so he begins to be afraid. Learning is never what one expects. Every step of learning is a new task, and the fear the man is experiencing begins to mount mercilessly, unyieldingly. His purpose becomes a battlefield." [5]

~ ~

[1] C.G. Jung, Memories, Dreams, Reflections (New York, Vintage Books, 1965), 209.

[2] M. Scott Peck, The Road Less Traveled (New York, Simon & Schuster, 1978), 15-16.

[3] Thomas Merton, The Seven Storey Mountain (New York, Harcourt Brace Jovanovich, Publishers, 1976), 83.

[4] Carlos Casteneda, The Fire from Within (New York, Simon & Schuster, 1984), 157.

[5] Carlos Casteneda, The Teachings of Don Juan: A Yaqui Way of Knowledge (New York, Simon & Schuster, 1974), 83-84.

17 TRICKS

The lights of Los Angeles have begun to appear outside the window. I feel the airplane adjust its pitch and continue its descent into the city.

**

"What will you do now?" he asked me.

We walked south along the beach that stretches below the cliffs separating Santa Monica from the Pacific Ocean. The sun was just below the horizon — the sand already cold, the sky a darkening blue. A fog was gathering over the ocean, and a low fence of mist divided our world into two, unequal portions.

"I don't know," I answered. "I need to simplify my life, but I don't know how."

Years before I had watched helplessly as circumstances had played its tricks and changed his life. Now, as my life changed, I watched enviously as his earlier confusion and reluctance gave way to resolve, and transformed him into this quiet, enormously strong, man.

"You do know how." he laughed, "You have met your pinches tiranitos chiquititos; you have learned, but you refuse to act." [1]

I suddenly felt very uncomfortable. For years we had followed and admired the adventures of UCLA's most infamous student of anthropology. We took turns applying his lessons to our own lives.

> "A petty tyrant is a tormentor," he replied. "Someone who either holds the power of life and death over warriors or simply annoys them to distraction."
>
> ...
>
> "My benefactor used to say that the warrior who stumbles on a petty tyrant is a lucky one. He meant that you're fortunate if you come upon one in your path, because if you don't, you have to go out and look for one." [2]

He turned and looked into my eyes.

"I wish there were a way," he said, "that I could deliver your blows. You're my friend. I would like to see you have your chance for freedom."

I felt a chill in my body — terror and longing in the same breath.

"I'm doing all right," I answered.

"You still don't get it, do you." he laughed.

**

"Ladies and Gentlemen, the Captain has turned on the 'No Smoking' sign and asks that you extinguish all cigarettes and bring your seats to an upright position. We will be landing in Los Angeles in five minutes."

I look out the window of the aircraft. The lights below are very close.

**

How am I to live my life when I occupy a universe

whose most basic features are unknown to me? I remember with nostalgia an earlier time in which my world offered itself at face value. The wind was a moving mass of air; fire was a chemical reaction with predictable properties; the Earth was solid ground beneath my feet. I had been born sometime in the past, and was destined to die sometime in the future. In between was a brief moment of consciousness in which I could succeed or fail, be happy or sad, according to clearly laid out rules for manipulating clearly defined material objects.

I had been tricked into seeing the world in this way, of course, but I had been a willing accomplice. Time, repetition, and a lazy mind had stripped away all mystery to reveal a pleasant, if somewhat bewildered, young man.

Now I have been tricked into seeing the world a different way. Is this better?

**

The plane is on final approach and I feel a slight shudder as its landing gear moves down and into position. I watch the city's lights rise to meet me until, inexplicably, the engine sounds change. The plane rises back into the heights; moves swiftly past the airport, and heads out over the ocean.

**

"It is the premise of many religions," my professor said, "that the world is inherently supernatural.

"Consider these words of a Trappist monk," he opened a book on his desk.

> They were poor, they had nothing, and therefore they
> were free and possessed everything, and everything

they touched struck off something of the fire of divinity.

...

Day after day the round of the canonical hours brought them together and the love that was in them became songs as austere as granite and as sweet as wine. And they stood and they bowed in their long, solemn psalmody. Their prayer flexed its strong sinews and relaxed again into silence, and suddenly flared up again in a hymn, the color of flame, and died into silence: and you could barely hear the weak, ancient voice saying the final prayer. The whisper of the amens ran around the stones like sighs, and the monks broke up their ranks and half emptied the choir, some remaining to pray.

...

The thought of those monasteries, those remote choirs, those cells, those hermitages, those cloisters, those men in their cowls, the poor monks, the men who had become nothing, shattered my heart. [3]

"Such actions are incomprehensible to those of us in the material world. But in a supernatural frame of reference, these men and women take on an importance that is beyond measure."

He looked at me.

"Scientists," he said, "live with the unknown. There are others, I believe, who live with the unknowable."

A student near me asked, "Why would anyone want to live with the unknowable." He knocked his knuckles on his desk, "This is enough."

The professor looked at him, knocked his own knuckles against the wall, and laughed, "Not only does it appear to be enough, but it is so compelling that it often appears to be everything!

"When Jesus said that it was easier for a camel to pass through the eye of the needle than for a rich man to enter into heaven, I don't think he was making a moral judgment. Rather, he was making a very pragmatic statement about the nature of mystery.

"If you are surrounded by this," he knocked once again on the wall, "you can see nothing else, much less desire anything else."

"You want us all to become monks?" a student cried out.

"No," the professor said. "I doubt that any of us would survive it."

He looked wistfully out the window and across the long stretch of quadrangle that approached the campus chapel.

"To eschew all this is an almost impossible act for the unaided will," he looked back into the room. "To see those heights requires that we be tricked by Grace. Few of us will be so lucky."

**

"Ladies and Gentlemen, the Captain has asked me to advise you that there may be a small problem with this aircraft, and that, as a precaution, you should review the procedures for an emergency landing and evacuation.

"In a few moments we will circle back and begin a new approach towards Los Angeles International Airport. Although we expect our landing to be routine, we ask that, during landing, you lean forward in your seats, keep your head down, and hold tightly to your ankles. If this position is uncomfortable for you, you should place both hands on the seat in front of you and brace your head against your hands.

"You do not need to assume this position now; we will be circling over the ocean for another half hour. The cabin crew will be passing through the cabin to assist you in your preparations, and to answer any questions you may have."

Silence.

"Ladies and Gentleman, this is your Captain. Please

don't be alarmed. I'm quite certain that there is nothing seriously wrong with this aircraft, and that our landing will be uneventful. Up here in the cockpit, a single light on our control panel is malfunctioning. Unfortunately, that light is used to confirm that our landing gear is down and locked. I believe that our landing gear is fine, but we should be prudent. I apologize for this little scare; the cabin crew will answer any questions you may have."

Strange, I think, how the world can change so dramatically in a breath. I remember another change … years ago.

**

"Why are you here?" she asked. "How can I help you?"

We sat facing each other across a low table. There was a large box of tissues on the table.

I won't cry, I told myself.

"I've been depressed for some time now, Doctor. Nothing I do seems able to shake it."

"How serious is this depression?" she asked. "Do you have thoughts of suicide?"

"No," I answered. "But I'm comforted by the fact that the option is always there."

"Depression is often a sign that you're ready to grow into a new life," she mused.

"Unlikely, in my case," I answered.

"Tell me about …" she began.

**

"KEEP YOUR HEAD DOWN. … BRACE. … KEEP YOUR HEAD DOWN. … BRACE. … KEEP …"

A stewardess is shouting these words from the back of

the cabin. I feel strangely calm. Locked in this private world about my knees, I hold my ankles and experience the world with exquisite clarity. I feel the seat in front of me with the top of my head; I feel my knees secured comfortably together by the blanket wrapped tightly around them; I hear the apparently normal sounds of the aircraft in this single moment before touchdown.

Touchdown.

The plane decelerates.

I breathe.

Sitting up, I look out the window to see the fire trucks racing with us as we speed down the runway.

Behind me a little girl talks excitedly with her mother.

"Did you see the angels, Mommy? There were angels in the clouds."

"Yes, dear, I saw them," her mother answers.

I breathe again.

~~

[1] Spanish for "teensy-weensy petty tyrants." See Carlos Casteneda, The Fire from Within (New York, Simon & Schuster, 1984), 30.

[2] Carlos Casteneda, The Fire from Within (New York, Simon & Schuster, 1984), 30-32.

[3] Thomas Merton, The Seven Storey Mountain (New York, Harcourt Brace Jovanovich, Publishers, 1976), 317-318.

18 LOVE

My automobile is rapidly losing power as I pull into the service station. My meetings over, I'm still several hundred miles from home. I stop the car next to the small office and look nervously towards these people who now hold my fate in their hands. A weathered, middle-aged man looks up from his desk and watches me from behind a large plate glass window. He shouts something I cannot hear and a younger man, perhaps his son, steps out of the service bay and walks toward me.

Both of them look Middle Eastern, and they possess the confident eyes and easy manner of assured businessmen.

"May I help you?" the young man asks.

**

My undergraduate college presented a wall of dark stone buildings that faced west along the top of a low cliff that rose above a sprawl of inexpensive but neatly kept single-family homes. At the base of this cliff was a diner that served as a second home for students who had not joined a fraternity and who chose not to eat in the college dining halls.

The owner of this diner was a large man who spent his days laughing in front of a low counter from which he served meals of limited variety but enormous size. I never noticed it at the time, but he always looked carefully into the eyes of every student that entered the diner. Usually he would just shout a request for an order from his grill; sometimes he would stop what he was doing, walk around the counter, sit down and speak quietly with his customer for just a moment.

> However, I did not bring up the subject of Murat in order to talk about this statue, but about M. and Mme. Privat. They were the people with whom we boarded, and long before we got to Murat, when the train was climbing up the snowy valley, from Aurillac, on the other side of the Puy du Cantal, Father was telling me: "Wait until you see the Privats."
>
> In a way, they were to be among the most remarkable people I ever knew.
>
> ...
>
> It is a great pleasure for me to remember such good and kind people and to talk about them. I just remember their kindness and goodness to me, and their peacefulness and their utter simplicity. They inspired real reverence, and I think, in a way, they were certainly saints. And they were saints in that most effective and telling way, sanctified by leading ordinary lives in a completely supernatural manner, sanctified by obscurity, by usual skills, by common tasks, by routine, but skills, tasks, routine which received a supernatural form from grace within, and from the habitual union of their souls with God in deep faith and charity. [1]

**

"Pull it into the service bay," the young man says. "We'll have a look."

I start the engine and drive my car carefully between two posts and into the cleanest work area I have ever seen. The tools are neatly racked and shining. The car next to mine has a cloth draped over its fender where a mechanic leans to adjust some inner mystery.

I climb out of my car to see the older man still sitting at his desk and listening intently to a young woman standing near the door. The woman holds one child in her right arm, and tethers another with her left. When the woman finishes speaking he holds up his hand, smiles, and walks into the garage where I am standing.

"Be with you in a moment," he says, and walks into a back office to speak with an old man in a dark suit who seems to be reading quietly and reverently from an old, leather-bound book.

Leaving this office he looks cordially at me once again and then finds that the path to his office is blocked by an old woman holding a bag of home grown vegetables. They speak earnestly in a language I do not understand as he tries to refuse the gift she thrusts at him. Finally, he accepts the gift gracefully and the woman, her mission completed, leaves the shop satisfied.

"Be with you in a moment," he says to me again as he reenters his office. He speaks to the young woman and I can see that although she is crying she seems also to be relieved. He pats her gently on the collar of her coat, touches the heads of each of her children, and walks back into the garage toward me.

"Let's have a look," he says.

**

"Are you still thinking about seminary?" the priest asked.

I stood with him in the Sacristy as he enrobed for the morning service. I was already dressed in the simple cassock and surplice of an altar boy. I didn't know what to say, because I had never thought about seminary.

"It's all right," the old man answered himself. "These things take time. Meanwhile, I've heard about this college … I have the information here somewhere …"

**

"Doesn't look too bad," the man says. "Have you back on the road in a minute."

I watch his hands. His long fingers play my engine block as a musical instrument. No wasted motion … everything straightforward and to the point.

Outside, his son talks to the driver of a sandwich truck that has broken down nearby. The driver holds his hands wide, his expression helpless.

The young man walks into the back office to confer with the old man and his book.

**

"How's college?" the priest asked.

His hands had the fine tremor of someone with early Parkinson's disease, and the diocese recently had given him an assistant to help him with the Mass. There's too much to do, he had told them. I can't retire yet.

"Fine," I said.

"And?" he asked.

"I've fallen in love with biology," I answered. "I'd like to go to graduate school instead of seminary."

Now my hands were shaking.

He looked up at me with shining eyes.

"That's marvelous! I'm proud of you!!" he said and meant it. "But you must still remember your ministry."

I stood there mute, confused.

"Everyone with a real life has a ministry."

"Who's in my congregation?" I asked, half in jest.

"Who's in your address book?" he answered seriously.

**

"All fixed," the man and his son say together.

"Thanks," I say. "How much do I owe you?"

"No parts," the younger man answers, "Just labor. Twenty dollars should do it."

I thank him, give him the money, and return to my car.

"Enjoy your trip," they call after me.

> As anyone could tell who had heard the songs Mr. Jonas made up as he passed, he was no ordinary junkman. To all appearances, yes, the way he dressed in tatters of moss-corduroy and the felt cap on his head, covered with the old presidential campaign buttons going back before Manila Bay. But he was unusual in this way: not only did he tread the sunlight, but often you could see him and his horse swimming along the moonlit streets, circling and recircling by night the islands, the blocks where all the people lived he had known all of his life.
>
> ...
>
> So it happened that often he was the only man alive in all Green Town at three in the morning and often people with headaches, seeing him amble by with his moon-shimmered horse, would run out to see if by any chance he had aspirin, which he did. More than once he had delivered babies at four in the morning and only then had people noticed how incredibly clean his hands and fingernails were — the hands of a rich man who had another life somewhere they could not guess.[2]

~~

[1] Thomas Merton, The Seven Storey Mountain (New York, Harcourt Brace Jovanovich, Publishers, 1976), 55–56.

[2] Ray Bradbury, Dandelion Wine (Garden City, Doubleday & Company, Inc.,1957), 246.

19 GRACE

I walk into the psychiatrist's office and sit in my usual chair. She sits opposite me and remains silent. Once seated, the first words are always mine.

"I'm behaving differently these days," I say.

Silence.

"Perfectly good old habits don't work anymore; I'm being forced to change my life in areas that are irrelevant to the things we talk about in here."

Silence.

"Well … maybe not irrelevant, but I'm complicating my life unnecessarily."

Silence.

"Actually, my life is becoming much simpler."

Laughter.

"It is funny," I say. "'Seek enlightenment through loss.' A curious slogan."

**

"What do you mean," the student asked, "when you say 'tricked by Grace?'"

"What I mean," my professor answered, "depends on

who you are. If you are religious then I mean that God —
in the form of the Holy Spirit for Christians — moves
through the lives of some people in mysterious ways to
help them in their journey towards God. If you are not
religious — but are nevertheless a decent and sensitive sort
of person — then I mean that the projections of the
unconscious move through the lives of some people in
mysterious ways to help them in their journey towards
sanity."

"That's crazy," the student complains.

"That's life," my professor answers.

**

"Are you happy?" she asks.

"No," I answer. "In some ways I'm more unhappy than
ever. These changes in my life have forced me to look at
myself and to see how weak I really am. For the first time I
realize that there are pieces of me scattered everywhere —
in the past, in other people's lives. I have no center."

"Did you ever have a center," she asks.

"No, not that I can remember," I say. "But I didn't
know it. I always thought that I was strong."

> The entire historical life of the figure Jesus of
> Nazareth was important for the Christians of the first
> centuries, but it was mainly his passion and his
> resurrection that were of decisive significance.
>
> ...
>
> The cross and the death of Christ became
> cornerstones of Christian spirituality, in that they made
> clear from the start that the way to God passes through
> the "narrow gate" (Matt 7:13) of suffering, humiliation,
> and service, and not through domination and power.
> Only when Christians are "weak" can they be really
> "strong" (Matt 6:39); capacity is identical with incapacity,
> with loss of one's soul (Matt 6:39), of one's very life.
> Christian spirituality was based on accepting as one's

own the very scandal of the crucified Son of Man, an acceptance that could lead to suffering and death, to martyrdom. It was not, therefore, an easy and uncostly spirituality. [1]

**

"For creatures with free will, to be tricked by Grace is only a beginning," mused my professor. "If we're lucky, trickery brings us to an insight into the 'true order of goods and of specific actions that ought to be accomplished or avoided.' [2] In pre-Reformation Christian theology, Grace shows us the path; but to achieve the 'kingdom of God' we must still do the work of walking that path."

"What do you mean," I asked, "'the work of walking that path.'"

"Life consists of problems to be solved," he answered. "If you face them — and the suffering invariably associated with them — you are walking the path, and you are growing spiritually. If you fail to face them, however, you must build a world of fantasy within which you can avoid your problems. These fantasies inevitably bear down on you, shrink you and eat away at your soul.

"Carl Jung wrote that 'Neurosis is always a substitute for legitimate suffering.' The Christian message is the same. [3] Many of you, no doubt, still hold to the notion that religion is a tissue work of lies designed to protect you from harsh reality. Reality is indeed harsh, but I would submit to you that it is religion — with its formalized experience of millennia of struggling, conscious beings — that can help you to avoid your own lies, face reality, and grow.

**

"Our hour is up," the psychiatrist says.

"Then I should go back to work," I answer.

~~

[1] John D. Zizioulas, "The Early Christian Community" In: Bernard McGinn, John Meyendorff, and Jean Leclercq, ed. Christian Spirituality: Origins to the Twelfth Century (New York, Crossroad, 1985), 24.

[2] J. Patout Burns, "Grace: The Augustinian Foundation" In: Bernard McGinn, John Meyendorff, and Jean Leclercq, ed. Christian Spirituality: Origins to the Twelfth Century (New York, Crossroad, 1985), 343.

[3] C.G. Jung, Psychology and Religion: West and East (Princeton, Princeton University Press, 1973), 75.

20 YEARS PASS

Years pass …

21 REMEMBERING

I sit on a sofa looking at a manuscript I wrote long ago. "The Only Real House of Mirrors" it says. It's midafternoon and the coffee table supports a vase of flowers, a cup of tea and a few magazines. I hear soft noises from another room.

"It's been so long," I muse, "and change comes so slowly. Did I really think it would be easy?"

**

I leave home and drive down to the beach. It's a cool, bright day and the beach is almost empty. I walk down the steps from the pier and step barefoot onto the cool sand. The world is divided into two parts. On my left is the ocean; the tide is coming in and the water rushes up to my feet and then pulls back – inviting me to follow. On my right the sand rises to a parking lot and to the city beyond.

An old couple has laid out a blanket near the stairs. He appears to be reading a technical book — each page is filled with mathematical notation — and she is writing something in a loose-leaf notebook. They both look up and smile. I return their smile and feel a warm glow deep in my chest. I start to walk towards them but then stop. "Not yet," I think.

I walk along the beach for almost an hour. I remember my years as a scientist when my technical knowledge was clear and precise in my mind; when new knowledge came to me every day – sometimes from a book and sometimes from the devices scattered about my laboratory. I remember my struggles with science and with the religious faith that had always been so deeply personal and serious for me. Such faith had returned and departed many times in my life. Each return brought with it new insights to be tested and often discarded. Each departure was marked by loss – an emptiness that grew ever so slightly with the passing years.

Long ago I had encountered a family running an auto repair shop hundreds of miles to the north. They had seemed so balanced -- both their day to day work and their inner faith merged in a fashion that I could only envy. Nevertheless, as my life changed and the passions of that earlier life dimmed, other opportunities arose to replace them. "Not so bad," I smiled.

**

Shortly after leaving the university I remember spending a Sunday afternoon worrying about my future and clinging painfully to the past. I had lost a good many of my friends with my departure from the university; I don't remember who stopped calling first.

The phone rang and, when I answered, I found myself talking to an acquaintance I knew only slightly.

"I understand that you're available to pursue new opportunities," he said. "I have some ideas, and I thought we might have lunch on Monday. Are you free?"

**

I turn back towards the pier. As I approach the stairs I look for the old couple, but they're gone. "Not yet," I smile.

**

I return to my home and read quietly until late in the evening. The book I'm reading tells of an artist who thought that her art had been amputated with her hand. It was given to me by a friend when I was quite young. She had so much to tell me; I was able to hear so little. She gave me four books — in desperation.

"Here," she said. "Read these! You need to read these!!"

I tried to read them, but could never get past the first few pages of the first volume. Years later I found them on my bookshelf and tried again.

"You did not recognize it, did you? I mean the handwriting on the envelope? I confess that I chuckled as I addressed it to you, before beginning this letter; I could see your face all of a sudden with its expression of perplexity. I saw you turn the letter over in your fingers for a moment trying to guess who had sent it!

"It is the first serious letter I have attempted, apart from short notes, with my new hand: this strange accessory-after-the-fact with which the good Amaril has equipped me! I wanted it to become word-perfect before I wrote to you. Of course I was frightened and disgusted by it at first, as you can imagine. But I have come to respect it very much, this delicate and beautiful steel contrivance which lies beside me so quietly on the table in its green velvet glove! Nothing falls out as one imagines it. I could not have believed myself accepting it so completely — steel and rubber seem such strange allies for human flesh. But the hand has proved itself almost more competent even than an ordinary flesh-and-blood member! In fact its powers are so comprehensive that I am a little frightened of it. It can undertake the most delicate of tasks, even turning the pages of a book, as well as the coarser ones. But most important of all — ah! Darley I tremble as I write the words — IT can paint!

"I have crossed the border and entered into the possession of my kingdom, thanks to the Hand. Nothing about this was premeditated. One day it took up a brush and lo! pictures of truly troubling originality and authority were born. I have five of them now. I stare at them with reverent wonder. Where did they come from? But I know that the Hand was responsible. And this new handwriting is also one of its new inventions, tall and purposeful and tender. Don't think that I boast. I am speaking with the utmost objectivity, for I know that I am not responsible. It is the Hand alone which has contrived to slip me through the barriers into the company of the Real Ones ..." [1]

So many of my friends have left time bombs in my life! — Books or ideas or memories that ignite in my brain years after their planting.

I lay down the book and think of my friend.

I walk down the short hallway to seek my wife and I notice a closet door slightly open. Instead of closing it, I look inside and find a backpack, tent, sleeping bag, and even some old climbing gear.

My wife is standing beside me. "A long time ago," she says. "Yes," I answer.

"Would you like to visit again?" she asks. "I wouldn't know how to get there," I answer.

"Step by step," she smiles.

~~

[1] Lawrence Durrell, Clea (New York, Pocket Books, 1960), 271–272.

22 RETURNING

I pull into the parking lot in front of the ranger station. I notice an old Volkswagen bug parked at the side of the building. I walk inside and approach the counter where a woman, a ranger, sits reading a book.

She looks up inquisitively.

"Can I help you?" she smiles.

For a moment I can't speak. The woman, the room, the light outside — in a moment I relive a lifetime of memories.

"I … a permit. I'd like a hiking permit," I stutter.

She points to the map beneath the glass plate of the counter.

"Where will you be hiking?" she asks.

I point to a trail.

She looks at me — catching and holding my eyes for a long moment.

"I would suggest this trail instead," she says, pointing to the map. "It takes a little longer, but it's worth it."

I want to argue, but something stops me.

I pay for the permit and, somewhat bewildered, head for the door.

"Enjoy your trip," she calls after me.

I drive to the trailhead, remove my gear, close and lock my car.

I look around the empty parking lot, take a deep breath, and then hoist my pack to my back.

She warned me that the trailhead was not well marked and even with her instructions it takes time to find.

"There it is," I say. "It looks easy enough."

I take my first step on the path.

EPILOG

It's early afternoon as I hike into this high meadow and see the glacier. I've been alone on the trail for days but now, suddenly, there are carnival tents! She never said anything about this!

A barker sits in his cage and eyes me with a smile.

"What is this place?" I ask.

He points to red lettering on a bright yellow banner that announces: "The Only Real House of Mirrors." Smaller, black letters say, "Enter at your own risk."

"How much?" I ask.

He points to another sign.

"That's a lot," I complain.

Silence.

I pay the barker his fee, enter, and follow the tent curtains along a twisting passage. It's dark. Up ahead I see an exit at the back of the tent.

"That's it?"

Feeling chagrined I leave the tent and follow a path up towards the ice.

I look back only once; the tents are gone.

AFTERWARDS

When I first began to show this book to my friends and to professional reviewers, many were confused.

"What is it?"

"Why did you write it?"

"Did it really happen?"

The answers are, "I don't know. I needed to. I think so."

The last question and answer — did it really happen? I think so. — deserves further words.

I was once a professional scientist who tried to keep both feet planted firmly on the ground. When I left science thirty-two years ago — a personal and professional crisis of some magnitude — I found myself adrift on an ocean of visions and voices that came unbidden to help me chart a course into a new and very different life.

The experiences described in this book actually happened. I don't, however, know how to separate the parts that actually happened inside my head from the parts that actually happened out there where you are.

There is a route up the side of a cliff in the Schawangunk's Reservation near New Paltz, New York that is called "Cascading Crystal Kaleidoscope." It is named after the confusing rush of images and distortions of time that technical rock climbers experience when they fall from the climb's most difficult point and arc across the face of the cliff on a journey determined by the length of the unanchored portion of their climbing rope.

This book is about such a fall, and about the utterly personal images that accompany such a fall. It is also about religious experience and about science.

Carl Jung once said, "What we are to our inward vision can only be expressed by way of myth. Myth is more individual and expresses life more precisely than does science."

For me, at least, this seems to be true!

David S. Barkley
Los Angeles, 2013

ABOUT THE AUTHOR

Dave Barkley (1943 -) was born in Austin, TX where he resided for two weeks. Ultimately he settled in Racine, WI until he moved to Hartford, CT to earn his B.S. at Trinity College. He then spent four years in the Biology Department at Princeton University where he earned an M.A. and Ph.D. in biology and biochemistry under the guidance of John T. Bonner and Malcolm S. Steinberg. He spent his early postdoctoral years in the Department of Neuropathology at Harvard Medical School before accepting a brief faculty position at the University of California, Los Angeles.

After publishing the "Dynamic Models ..." workbooks of electronic spreadsheet simulations in biochemistry, chemistry, and physics he began the task of moving these materials to a web based laboratory simulation called Virtlab which still lives at http://www.virtlab.com. It is an ongoing effort.

He resides in both Los Angeles, CA and Jakarta, INDONESIA with his wife Medias Pratiwi.

www.ingramcontent.com/pod-product-compliance
Lightning Source LLC
Chambersburg PA
CBHW071311130626
46556CB00004B/1565